FAIRY TALES

MOTHER GOOSE'S
FAIRY TALES

WITH OVER TWO HUNDRED ILLUSTRATIONS

BY

E. H. CORBOULD, ALFRED CROWQUILL, W. McCONNELL,

AND OTHERS

LP LONGMEADOW PRESS

1996

A Platinum Press Book

Library of Congress Cataloging-in-Publication Data

Mother Goose.
    Mother Goose's fairy tales / with illustrations by John Gilbert ...
[et al.].
        p. cm.
    "A Platinum Press book."
    Earlier 1895 ed. has title: Mother Goose's nursery rhymes and
fairy tales.
    Summary: An illustrated collection of twenty fairy tales
including "Jack and the Beanstalk," "Ali Baba and the Forty
Thieves," "Puss in Boots," and "The Ugly Duckling."
    1. Fairy tales. [1. Fairy tales. 2. Folklore]   I. Gilbert, John,
ill. II. Title.
    PZ8.M849mp   1995
    398.2 — dc20
    [E]   95-45996
                                             CIP
                                           AC

This special reprint edition, originally published
in 1895, is now republished by:

Longmeadow Press
201 High Ridge Road
Stamford, CT 06904

in association with

Platinum Press Inc.
311 Crossways Park Drive
Woodbury, NY 11797

Every attempt has been made to provide an
authentic facsimile edition. As the original 100-year-old
manuscript was used for reproduction,
the type quality reflects this.

Cover design by James C. Romano II

ISBN: 0-681-21633-6

Printed in USA

First Longmeadow Press Edition 1996

0 9 8 7 6 5 4 3 2 1

CONTENTS.

THE FIRST SIGHT OF THE GOLDEN EGG.

THE HISTORY OF OLD MOTHER GOOSE
AND HER SON JACK.

 I AM sure I could not tell you how long ago it is since Old Mother Goose lived in a cottage with her son Jack. But I know very well that the cottage was as pretty as any that you would ever wish to see. Woodbine and jessamine twined upwards in front of its walls, and roses bloomed there in red and white beauty for months together. It had a garden, too, and it was Jack's duty to attend to it all the year round. A very good lad was Jack, for he would work in this garden from morning till night, digging, pruning, and planting, till his arms ached, and till the sun scorched his face to the colour of a red fuchsia blossom.

Perhaps you would like to know what kind of lad Master Jack was. Well, I can hardly say that he was handsome; for when he laughed he would open his mouth and eyes to their utmost stretch, and the sound he uttered did not show him to be very wise. But this was only in his early youth. Still, he was a strong, hard-working, good-tempered lad, and if his gardening had made his hands

11

large and brown, his heart was tender, and full of love towards his

mother ; so you will think, as I do, that Jack was a very good lad

indeed. And if his hair would not curl, his skill in growing cabbages very fairly made up for the defect. Besides, his earnest work not

only gave him health and strength, but spread such a smile of satisfaction over his face, as made him look far handsomer than half the
other boys in the neighbourhood. And so thought Mother Goose
herself, who doted upon her son Jack.

Old Mother Goose's high-crowned hat was almost as tall as a
chimney-pot; and I am certain the stick which helped her to hobble
about was twice as long. A poppy was not redder than her gown
and the high heels of her shoes; while her apron and kerchief were
equal to the snowdrop for whiteness.

Then there was the gander that swam in the pond at a little
distance from the cottage. He kept up a constant "Qua-a-ak,
qua-a-ak!" from morning to night. I must not forget the owl,
which hung in a wicker cage by the side of the cottage window.

All day long would he sit upon his perch, with his head huddled

into his shoulders, looking very tired and sleepy, and cold and un-

happy. But at night he was sharp enough, and then his eyes were quicker than you would ever believe if you had only seen him by day. Old Mother Goose was quite aware of this, and trusted in her owl as a very good watchman during the night. "Qua-a-ak!" went the gander; and "Whit-tu-whoo, Tu-whit-tu-whoo!" cried the owl; Jack sprinkled the flower-beds, cropped the grass, and planted the potatoes; and Old Mother Goose, all the while, hobbled about with her long stick and her spring shoes with the high red heels.

So you see they all formed together a very happy family. But what a fine strong fellow was the gander! what a large yellow beak he had! and as for wings, there never was a gander that had so grand a pair. Whenever Old Mother Goose wanted to take a journey, she had only to tap, tap, with her stick at the edge of the pond, and straightway would Master Gander swim up to her.   Then she would mount upon his broad, strong back, and away, away would he fly, and carry her swifty to any distance.   I know well enough it is not a common thing for a gander to fly through the air, and

carry an old lady on his back ; but you must not forget that this gander was the most wonderful gander that was ever seen !

Now Old Mother Goose thought her gander often looked sad and lonely as he swam about in his pond ; so, one day, she called her son Jack to her, and told him to dress himself in his best jacket and collar, and to put on his fine new hat.

" My son Jack," she said to him, " I want you to leave the garden and the flowers for a day; you must go to market, and buy me the finest, the whitest, and the most yellow-beaked goose you can see.

The owl and I will mind the cottage. Make haste, my dear son, for I shall not be happy till I see the goose swimming in the pond."

Upon this, Jack set out on his journey to market. It was early morning when he started, and his way lay through a wood. Jack felt very happy as he wandered along; and as for fearing robbers,

or any other bad men who might attack him, why, Jack laughed at the very thought. I must tell you that Old Mother Goose, who never forgot anything, so prudent and careful was she, had armed Jack with her great clothes-prop. Throwing this weapon over his shoulder, Jack trudged along like a man—like a general at the head of an army, in fact.

The green trees, the flowing silver stream, and the songs of the birds in the fresh morning air, caused Jack's spirits to rise till he became more joyful than he had ever before been in his life. And in his happiness he began to loiter and to stroll out of the road. He left the road, and plunged into the thick of the beautiful trees which grew along its edge, now and then taking great leaps across ditches by means of his clothes-prop. He came down flat upon his back, though, once or twice; but he did not care for this, and as for his best jacket, he never bestowed a thought upon it. When he had fairly tired himself out with his walking and jumping, he began to think about seeking his proper way. And no sooner had he done so than he found out that he had lost himself in the wood. At first he sat down, and in his alarm shed tears; but his courage soon returned, and he tried to recall the path he had taken since he left

the road. It was all in vain! He knew not whether to turn to the right hand or to the left. At length he thought of a plan: he would climb up one of the high trees, and from a topmost branch look out for the road.

He then went up to the nearest tree, and after great labour reached its lowest branch, and from that up to the next; but in trying the third, he had to stretch out very far to reach it: of course he bent forward, but no sooner had he done so than he missed his footing, and fell flat upon the ground. Still he kept on trying to ascend the tree. Again and again he got up, only to reach the grass beneath

a great deal faster than he mounted. Once he had a narrow escape
of being very much hurt; for, on reaching a high branch, he slipped,
and toppling over, hung for a long time by one leg bent over the

bough. He managed, however, to get down, but not without scratching his face and hands with the twigs, and having his clothes torn in many places.

After he had made many attempts to climb the tree, and as he was lying on the ground very much shaken by his last fall, he heard a scream at a little distance from where he was. He jumped up directly, and throwing his clothes-prop over his shoulder, he ran with the boldness of a brave young fellow, towards the spot. Through an opening in the trees he saw a lovely young lady struggling with a great brutal fellow, who was trying to snatch her fine silken mantle from her shoulders. Quick as thought, and long before the rascal was aware of it, Jack had planted his staff, with all his might, upon

the arms, legs, back, and head of the wicked fellow; and by one very heavy blow he sent the rogue howling away as fast as his legs would carry him. Jack then returned to the young lady, who was lying on the ground weeping; he raised her gently, and soothed her by telling her not to fear, as the robber was soundly beaten, and had made off. The lady soon dried her tears, and thanked Jack for having saved her from being robbed. As for Jack, he had never seen so beautiful a young lady before; and he felt as though he would like to use his clothes-prop twenty times a day upon a robber's back, in order to earn the thanks of so graceful a creature. The young lady told Jack that she was the daughter of the Squire whose great white house on the hill-top he had often looked at with wonder. She knew the path out of the wood quite well; and as she led him through the forest she told him how she had heard the robber talk-

ing with two others of going to the market to steal a wonderful
goose, which would enrich its owner, and which was to be sold that
day.   When she reached the border of the forest, she pointed out

the way to Jack, and invited him to her father's house, in order that
he might thank Jack for his noble conduct.

Now, when Jack was left alone, he could not help thinking that
the wonderful goose of which the young lady had spoken must be
the one his mother had meant he should bring home to her. This
fancy added a greater pleasure to that which he had already felt at
having done a noble deed. And he hastened forward as fast as his
legs would take him, so as to reach the market-place before the
robbers—who desired, like himself, to possess the valuable goose—
should get there. I must tell you that Jack had little trouble in
picking out the best goose in the market, for, when he reached it, it
was very late, and there was but one goose left for sale. This goose
was a prime one: as white in its plumage, and as yellow-beaked, as
his mother could desire. Jack bought it at once, and this time
keeping to the road, made straight for home.

But his journey was not without some little mishaps. The yellow-
beaked goose seemed greatly to object to being carried; and she
cried "Qua-a-ak, qua-a-ak!" till Jack dropped her from underneath
his arm. Afterwards, when she had walked slowly and gravely
along for a short time, she would again cry "Qua-a-ak, qua-a-ak!"
and then stand stock-still, staring up at Jack with the most comical

expression. Once she tried to fly away; so Jack was forced to seize her in his arms, and to keep her there till he reached home.

The delight of Old Mother Goose was great indeed when she saw what a fine bird Jack had bought. As for the gander, he showed more joy than I could describe. He sailed round and round her as she swam in the pond, picked up the morsels out of the water for his new friend, and led the way to that part of the pond where the food was richest and daintiest. But the old owl grew jealous at the sight of the beautiful goose. He buried his head still deeper in his shoulders, and looked colder and more mopish and sleepy than ever;

and I have no doubt he slept night and day for a week out of sheer envy.

And then Old Mother Goose, and Jack, and the gander, and his

companion lived a peaceful, happy life for a long time.   Yet often
would Jack cease his work to dream about the face of the lovely lady
whom he had rescued in the forest ; and often would he, out of pure
absence of mind, strike his spade right into the midst of his best
flower-beds.   Jack soon began to sigh all day long.   He neglected
the garden ; the sight of the gander no longer pleased him ; and
even the beautiful goose was scarcely noticed by him.

   But the goose was soon to reward him for all his former kindness,
though he now seemed to regard her as unworthy of a thought.   One

morning, as he was walking along the edge of the pond, he saw both
the goose and gander wagging their beaks, and chattering away as
if they were in the utmost glee. He went up to them, and what
was his astonishment at finding, lying on the bank, a large, glittering
golden egg! When the joyous couple in the pond saw him pick up
the egg, and regard it with such a delighted air, their beak-clapping
and head-wagging became still greater, and as they watched him
run towards his mother's cottage, the pond resounded with their
gleeful " Qua-a-ak, qua-a-ak's !" Old Mother Goose told her son
it was indeed an egg of pure gold that their goose had given them.

" Go to market, my son," the old woman said ; " sell your egg, and
you will be rich enough to pay a visit up yonder !"

And Old Mother Goose pointed with her stick in the direction of
the Squire's fine white house which crowned the hill-top. She knew
very well that it was her son's love for the Squire's lovely daughter
that had caused him to destroy so many flower-beds with his spade.

So to market Jack went, and sold his golden egg ; but I must tell
you that poor Jack got only half his due from the rogue who bought
it from him. Jack did not know this, though, at the time ; and his

new-found riches made him bold. He dressed himself in his finest suit, and went to the Squire's house. When he got there, two foot-men stood at the door, the one looking very stout and saucy, and the other sleepy and stupid. When Jack asked to see the Squire,

they sneered at him, and then amused themselves by making sport of his fine suit of clothes, and laughing outright at the redness of his face; but as to taking a message to the Squire, it was too ridiculous to be thought of, the one being too proud and idle, and the other too lazy, till Jack had wit enough to offer them each a guinea, when they both became active and civil, showing him to the Squire's room at once, without even asking for his card.

Now the Squire, who was very rich, was also very proud and very fat : in fact, as much puffed up as plenty of money, plenty of ease, rich living, port wine, and hot suppers could make him. Of course he scarcely turned his head to notice Jack when he entered the room ; and when he began to explain his errand, the Squire listened with so lofty an air, that he seemed to be going to sleep. But when Jack showed him his bag of gold, and asked for his daughter to be

his bride, the Squire laughed at him, and ordered his servants to seize him, and throw him into the horse-pond.

It was not so easy, though, thus to dispose of Jack. He was an active young fellow, and many of the people who laid hands on him were felled to the earth by his stout clothes-prop. But when the

lovely young lady came out, and with tears besought her father to release poor Jack from his tormentors, Jack grew more deeply in love with her than ever, and went home, with his clothes torn it is true, but not the less determined to win her for a wife for all that.

And well did his precious goose aid him in his design. Almost every morning would she lay him a golden egg; and Jack, grown wiser, would no longer sell them at half their value to the rogue who had before cheated him. It was not long ere Jack grew to be a richer man, thanks to his goose, than the Squire himself. His wealth soon became known to all the country round, and the Squire at length consented to accept Jack as his son-in-law.

But a great misfortune had well-nigh happened to Jack a short

time before his marriage-day. One night the rogue, to whom Jack

had sold his golden egg, came by stealth to the pond, and seized

the beautiful goose.   He brought with him a sharp knife, intending
to cut open the poor goose's stomach, and so obtain all the golden
treasure which he foolishly fancied was contained therein.   I need
not tell you how silly he was for supposing that to be the best mode
of securing the golden eggs.   But I must inform you how his wicked
design was thwarted.   He had seized the goose, and was about to
carry her off and kill her, when the old owl set up so loud a screech
that the gander awoke, and began to "Qua-a-ak!" and Old Mother
Goose jumped out of bed in affright, and Jack instantly ran out, and
first of all rescued his goose, and then soundly thrashed the rogue
with the clothes-prop.   The rascal made off as quickly as his feet
could touch the ground, and this being the second drubbing he had
received at the hands of the brave Jack, he took good care not to
come in his way any more.   Perhaps you will think with me, that
this piece of timely warning was quite enough to cause Jack to for-
give the old owl for all his moping, and envy of the beautiful goose.

Jack now arrived at the very height of his happiness, for he was
married to the lovely daughter of the Squire, who was himself present, in all his pride and pomp, at the ceremony; and the bells rang
gaily, and the people (who were proud of Jack, as one of themselves,
and who admired the beautiful bride and her fine clothes) shouted
and waved their handkerchiefs as they came out of the church ; and
the footmen who had sneered at Jack in earlier days were now
obliged to attend upon him : he had the generosity to take no notice
of their former insolence.

And where was Old Mother Goose? Why, she stayed at home to get ready the house for the new-married couple, and when she had welcomed them to their new home she flew away into the woods

on the back of her strong gander, leaving the cottage and the goose to Jack and his bride, who had a family of children as handsome as their mother and as brave as their father, and lived happily ever afterwards.

ALADDIN, AND THE WONDER-FUL LAMP.

———o———

ALADDIN was the son of a poor tailor in an Eastern city. He was a spoiled boy, and loved play better than work ; so that when Mustapha, his father, died, he was not able to earn his living ; and his poor mother had to spin cotton all day long to procure food for their support. But she dearly loved her son, knowing that he had a good heart, and she believed that as he grew older he would do better, and become at last a worthy and prosperous man. One day, when Aladdin was walking outside the town, an old man came up to him, and looking very hard in his face, said he was his father's brother, and had long been away in a distant country, but that now he wished to help his nephew to get on. He then put a ring on the boy's finger, telling him that no harm could happen to him so long as he wore it. Now, this strange man was no uncle of Aladdin, nor was he related at all to him ; but he was a wicked Magician, who wanted to make use of the lad's services, as we shall see presently.

The old man led Aladdin a good way into the country.

until they came to a very lonely spot between two lofty black mountains. Here he lighted a fire, and threw into it some gum, all the time repeating many strange words. The ground then opened just before them, and a stone trap-door appeared. After lifting this up, the Magician told Aladdin to go below, down some broken steps, and at the foot of these he would find three halls, in the last of which was a door leading to a garden full of beautiful trees ; this he was to cross, and after mounting some more steps, he would come to a terrace, when he would see a niche, in which there was a lighted lamp. He was then to take the lamp, put out the light, empty it of oil, and bring it away with him.

Aladdin found all the Magician had told him to be true : he passed quickly but cautiously through the three halls, so as not even to touch the walls with his clothes, as the Magician had directed. He took the lamp from the niche, threw out the oil, and put it in his bosom. As he came back through the garden, his eyes were dazzled with the bright-coloured fruits on the trees, shining like glass. Many of these he plucked and put in his pockets, and then returned with the lamp, and called upon his uncle to help him up the broken steps.

"Give me the lamp," said the old man, angrily.

"Not till I get out safe!" cried the boy.

The Magician, in a passion, then slammed down the trap-door, and Aladdin was shut up fast enough. While crying bitterly, he by chance rubbed the ring, and a figure appeared before him, saying,

" I am your slave, the Genius of the Ring ; what do you desire ? "

Aladdin told the Genius of the Ring that he only wanted to be set free, and to be taken back to his mother. In an instant he found himself at home, very hungry, and his poor mother was much pleased to see him again. He told her all that had happened ; she then felt curious to look at the lamp he had brought, and began rubbing it, to make it shine brighter. Both were quite amazed at seeing rise before them a strange figure ; this proved to be the Genius of the Lamp, who asked for their commands. On hearing that food was what they most wanted, a black slave instantly entered with the choicest fare upon a dainty dish of silver, and with silver plates for them to eat from.

Aladdin and his mother feasted upon the rich fare brought to them, and sold the silver dish and plates, on the produce of which they lived happily for some weeks. Aladdin was now able to dress well, and in taking his usual walk, he one day chanced to see the Sultan's daughter coming with her attendants from the baths. He was so much struck with

her beauty, that he fell in love with her at once, and told his mother that she must go to the Sultan, and ask him to give the Princess to be his wife. The poor woman said he must be crazy ; but her son not only knew what a treasure he had got in the magic lamp, but he had also found how valuable were the shining fruits he had gathered, which he thought at the time to be only coloured glass. At first he sent a bowlful of these jewels—for so they were—to the Sultan, who was amazed at their richness, and said to Aladdin's mother,

"Your son shall have his wish, if he can send me in a week, forty bowls like this, carried by twenty white and twenty black slaves, handsomely dressed."

He thought by this to keep what he had got, and to hear no more of Aladdin. But the Genius of the Lamp soon brought the bowls of jewels and the slaves, and Aladdin's mother went with them to the Sultan.

The Sultan was overjoyed at receiving these rich gifts, and at once agreed that the Princess Bulbul should be the wife of Aladdin. The happy youth then summoned the Genius of the Lamp to assist him, and shortly set out for the palace. He was dressed in a handsome suit of clothes, and rode a beautiful horse : by his side marched a number of attendants, scattering handfuls of gold among the people. As soon as

they were married, Aladdin ordered the Genius of the Lamp to build, in the course of a night, a most superb palace, and there the young couple lived quite happily for some time. One day, when Aladdin was out hunting with the Sultan, the wicked Magician, who had heard of his good luck, and wished to get hold of the magic lamp, cried out in the streets, "New lamps for old ones!" A silly maid in the palace, hearing this, got leave of the Princess to change Aladdin's old lamp, which she had seen on a cornice where he always left it, for a new one, and so the Magician got possession of it.

As soon as the Magician had safely got the lamp, he caused the Genius to remove the palace, and Bulbul within it, to Africa. Aladdin's grief was very great, and so was the rage of the Sultan at the loss of the Princess, when he had got over his wonder at the disappearance of the palace; and poor Aladdin's life was in some danger, for the Sultan threatened to kill him if he did not restore his daughter in three days. Aladdin first called upon the Genius of the Ring to help him, but all he could do was to take him to Africa. The Princess was rejoiced to see him again, but was very sorry to find that she had been the cause of all their trouble by parting with the wonderful lamp. Aladdin, however, consoled her, and told her that he had thought of

a plan for getting it back. He then left her, but soon returned with a powerful sleeping-draught, and advised her to
receive the Magician with pretended kindness, and pour it
into his wine at dinner that day, so as to make him fall
sound asleep, when they could take the lamp from him.
Everything happened as they expected ; the Magician drank
the wine, and when Aladdin came in, he found that he had
fallen back lifeless on the couch. Aladdin took the lamp
from his bosom, and called upon the Genius to transport the
palace, the Princess, and himself back to their native city.
The Sultan was as much astonished and pleased at their
return as he had been provoked ; and Aladdin, with his
Bulbul, lived long afterwards to enjoy his good fortune.

BLUE-BEARD.

————o————

ONCE upon a time there was a very rich man, who lived
in a castle. He had great quantities of gold and silver, and
precious stones and money; but he was very ugly, and had
a blue beard. And yet for all this, Blue-Beard had already
been married six times. As all his wives were dead, he
wished to marry again, and turned his thoughts to the family
of a lady in his neighbourhood, who had two beautiful
daughters. But neither of the young ladies would consent
to marry a man with a blue beard, more especially as his
former wives had all disappeared in a mysterious manner.
Blue-Beard, however, invited the family to his castle, and
entertained them all for a week in so magnificent a manner
that every one was charmed with him. He paid particular
attention to the younger of the two daughters, and was so
kind and gracious, that before the week was ended she had
consented to become his wife.

They had just been married one month when Blue-Beard
told his wife one morning, that urgent business called him

away from home. He said he hoped she would make herself happy in the meantime, and invite her friends to see her; and he gave her the keys of all the castle, of the rooms in which he kept his treasures, and of the chests which contained his money and jewels.

"You may examine everything," he said, "except one closet, which I call the *blue* chamber. I have particular reasons for not wishing this room to be seen; and if you disobey me you will incur my highest displeasure. This key opens the passage leading to the chamber, and this little key opens the chamber itself. I leave them with you, to prove to you that I have every confidence in your discretion."

The name of the wife was Fatima, and her sister's name was Anne. Anne was then staying with Fatima at the castle, and they thought it would be pleasant to have their two brothers there also, to keep them company while Blue-Beard was away. So they sent for them, and they promised to come the next day.

In the meantime, the sisters amused themselves in going over the castle, and looking at everything they had not seen before. But Fatima was constantly thinking of the blue chamber, and wondering why her husband did not wish her to see it; and at last her curiosity was so great that she could not resist it. She reached the closet, and with a

trembling hand put the little key into the lock, turned it, and pushed open the door. In her agitation the key fell upon the floor.

At first she could see nothing, for the room was quite dark; but what was her horror when she found the floor all covered with blood, and several dead bodies lying against the walls! These were Blue-Beard's former wives, who had disappeared, no one knew how, but who, it was now plain, had been barbarously murdered by their cruel husband With a shriek of terror she ran out of the chamber; but then she thought of the key, and therefore once more entered it, picked up the key, and rushed back to her own room.

After recovering a little from her fright, she looked at the key, and found a spot of blood upon it. This she carefully washed off, but there still remained a stain. She then took sand and rubbed the part; but, to her astonishment, the stain had re-appeared on the other side of the key. She rubbed again, but all in vain; as fast as she cleared it from one spot, it re-appeared on another; for, you must know, the key was a fairy key. At last she was forced to give it up in despair.

The next morning, to her great susprise and alarm, Blue-Beard suddenly returned, saying that he had received letters on the road, informing him that the business he went about

had been settled. Shortly afterwards he asked for his keys, and Fatima went to fetch them. On her return, he was walking in the garden, and she presented them to him with a trembling hand.

" I do not see here the key of the blue chamber," he said, sternly.

" I suppose I must have left it in my room," faltered Fatima.

" Bring it, then, immediately," said her husband, walking into the castle.

She saw that it was in vain for her to attempt any further excuses, so she brought down the fatal key.

" There is blood upon this key," said Blue-Beard, as soon as he looked at it. " How did it come there ? "

Fatima, trembling and confused, said she did not know.

" You do know, madam," said he, fiercely, "and I know too : you have opened the blue chamber against my orders. I hope you were pleased with what you saw there ; in another moment you will be there again ! "

He seized her by the hair, and dragged her along the ground ; she shrieked, and implored his forgiveness, but nothing would move him. At last she entreated him to grant her a few minutes to say her prayers, and to speak to her sister.

68

"I will give you one quarter of an hour," he said, "but not a moment longer."

She flew to her room, and begged her sister to run to the top of the tower and see if her brothers were coming.

Presently she called out, "Sister Anne! Sister Anne! Do you see any one coming?"

"I see nothing," said Anne, "but the scorching sun and the waving grass."

A few minutes later she again called out, "Anne! Sister Anne! Do you see any one coming?"

"I only see," replied Anne, "a great dust."

"Oh! is it my brothers?"

"Alas! no," said Anne, "I now see it is only a flock of sheep!"

Blue-Beard stood in the hall below, with his drawn scimitar in his hand.

"The time is up," he cried at last; "come down!"

"I am coming," said Fatima. Again she called to her sister, "Sister Anne! Sister Anne! Do you see any one coming?"

"I see two horsemen coming, but they are a great way off."

"God be praised!" said Fatima, "they are my brothers."

Then Blue-Beard once more cried out, in a voice of thunder

that made the whole castle ring, "Come down! or I will fetch you."

Fatima descended slowly, and threw herself at her husband's feet. "Oh! mercy!" she cried, "only for a little while."

"It is of no use," he said, "you must die!"

Again he seized her by the hair, and raised his arm to strike; but just at that moment the horn at the gate blew such a tremendous blast that he almost leaped from the ground with the start, and flinging Fatima aside, rushed out to see who it was. The gate opened, and two horsemen rode into the court. They were the brothers. Blue-Beard prepared to defend himself; but he was almost immediately slain. As he left no heirs, Fatima inherited all his wealth; and after a time she married again, and lived very happily.

CINDERELLA;

OR, THE LITTLE GLASS SLIPPER.

———o———

THERE was, many years ago, a gentleman who had a charming lady for his wife. They had one daughter only, who was very dutiful to her parents. But while she was still very young, her mamma died, to the grief of her husband and daughter. After a time, the little girl's papa married another lady. Now, this lady was proud and haughty, and had two grown-up daughters as disagreeable as herself; so the poor girl found everything at home changed for the worse.

But she bore all her troubles with patience, not even complaining to her father; and, in spite of her hard toil, she grew more lovely in face and figure every year.

Now, the King's son gave a grand ball, and all persons of quality were invited to it. Our two young ladies were not overlooked. Nothing was now talked of but the rich dresses they were to wear.

At last the happy day arrived. The two proud sisters set off in high spirits. Cinderella followed them with her eyes until the coach was out of sight. She then began to cry bitterly. While she was sobbing, her godmother, who was a Fairy, appeared before her.

"Cinderella," said the Fairy, "I am your godmother, and for the sake of your dear mamma I am come to cheer you up, so dry your tears. You shall go to the grand ball to-night, but you must do just as I bid you. Go into the garden and bring me a pumpkin."

Cinderella brought the finest that was there. Her godmother scooped it out very quickly, and then struck it with her wand, upon which it was changed

into a beautiful coach. Afterwards, the old lady peeped into the mouse-trap, where she found six mice. She tapped them lightly with her wand, and each mouse became a fine horse. The rat-trap contained two large rats; one of these she turned into a coachman, and the other into a postillion. The old lady then told Cinderella to go into the garden and seek for half a dozen lizards. These she changed into six footmen, dressed in the gayest livery.

When all these things had been done, the kind godmother, touching her with her wand, changed her worn-out clothes into a beautiful ball-dress, embroidered with pearls and silver. She then gave her a pair of glass slippers—that is, they were woven of the most delicate spun glass, fine as the web of a spider.

When Cinderella was thus attired, her godmother made her get into her splendid coach, giving her a caution to leave the ball before the clock struck twelve.

On her arrival, her beauty struck everybody with wonder. The gallant Prince gave her a courteous welcome, and led her into the ball-room; and the King and Queen were as much enchanted with her, as the Prince conducted her to the supper-table, and was too much occupied in waiting upon her to partake of anything himself. While seated, Cinderella heard the clock strike three-quarters past eleven. She rose to leave, the Prince pressing her to accept an invitation for the ball on the following evening.

On reaching home, her godmother praised her for being so punctual, and agreed to let her go to the next night's ball.

Although she seemed to be tired, her sisters, instead of showing pity, teased her with glowing accounts of the splendid scene they had just left, and spoke particularly of the beautiful Princess. Cinderella was delighted to hear all this, and asked them the name of the Princess, but they replied, nobody knew her. So much did they say in praise

of the lady, that Cinderella expressed a desire to go to the next ball to see the Princess; but this only served to bring out their dislike of poor Cinderella still more, and they would not lend her the meanest of their dresses.

The next evening the two sisters went to the ball, and Cinderella also, who was still more splendidly dressed than before. Her enjoyment was even greater than at the first ball, and she was so occupied with the Prince's tender sayings, that she was not so quick in marking the progress of time.

To her alarm she heard the clock strike twelve! In her haste she dropped one of her glass slippers, and reached home, out of breath, with none of her godmother's fairy gifts but one glass slipper.

When her sisters arrived after the ball, they spoke in terms of rapture of the unknown Princess, and told Cinderella about the little glass slipper she had dropped, and how the Prince picked it up. It was evident to all the Court that the Prince was deter-

82

mined, if possible, to find out the owner of the slipper; and a few days afterwards, a royal herald proclaimed that the King's son would marry her whose foot the glass slipper should be found exactly to fit.

This proclamation caused a great sensation. Ladies of all ranks were permitted to make a trial of the slipper; but it was of no use. Cinderella now said, "Let me try—perhaps it may fit me." It slipped on in a moment. Great was the vexation of the two sisters at this; but what was their astonishment when Cinderella took the fellow slipper out of her pocket!

At that moment the godmother appeared, and touched Cinderella's clothes with her wand. Her sisters then saw that she was the beautiful lady they had met at the ball, and, throwing themselves at her feet, craved her forgiveness.

A short time after she was married to the Prince, to the intense gratification of the whole Court.

ALI BABA AND THE FORTY THIEVES.

———o———

In a town in Persia lived two brothers—Cassim and Ali Baba. Cassim was rich, but Ali Baba was poor, and gained his living by cutting wood, and bringing it upon three asses into the town to sell.

One day he saw some robbers in a forest; he watched them from a hiding-place, and counted forty of them. They carried bags of treasure, and hid it in a cave, which opened for them in the solid rock on saying the words, "Open, Sesame." When they came out again, the captain said, "Shut, Sesame," and the door shut behind them, and they rode off.

Then Ali Baba came down from his hiding-place, and went to the rock, and said, "Open, Sesame,"

and a door opened, and he entered and found all manner of treasure : he carried off a quantity of gold coin, and lading his asses with it, went home. When he showed it to his wife, she wanted to measure it, to see how much they possessed, and she went to Cassim's wife to borrow a measure, and Cassim's wife lent it to her, putting some suet at the bottom of the measure.

Ali Baba and his wife then measured the gold, and buried it in the ground ; and when Cassim's wife received back the measure, she found a piece of gold sticking to the suet. She told Cassim, who persuaded his brother to tell him the secret of the cave, and went next day to get treasure for himself. He entered the cave by saying, " Open, Sesame ; " but when he was ready to depart, having gathered many bags together, he could not think of the magic words, and so was obliged to remain in the cave till the robbers returned, who, enraged at having their

secret discovered, killed him, and cut his body into four quarters, hanging them inside the cave.

Cassim's wife, finding that her husband did not return, went to tell Ali Baba, who at once set off to go to the cave, and on entering it discovered his brother's remains, which he carried home on one of his asses, loading the other two with bags of gold. Ali Baba then buried the body, and contrived, with the assistance of an intelligent slave named Mòrgiana, to make every one believe that Cassim had died a natural death, and soon became very rich and prosperous.

Meanwhile the forty robbers visited their cave, and finding that Cassim's body had been removed, determined not to rest until they had discovered their enemy ; and one of them undertaking the search, in which he was assisted by the cobbler who had sewn Cassim's body together, at last found Ali Baba's house, which he marked with a piece of chalk,

and then returned to his fellows. When Morgiana saw the mark, she chalked several other doors in the same manner. The thieves then coming to attack the house, and not being able to distinguish it from the others, had to return to their cave; and the robber, who they thought had misled them, was put to death.

Another robber then undertook the enterprise, and being guided by the cobbler, marked the door with red chalk; but Morgiana marked the neighbours' doors in the same manner, and so defeated them a second time; and the second robber was put to death. The captain then went into the town himself, and having found and carefully observed Ali Baba's house, returned to his men, and ordered them to buy nineteen mules and thirty-eight leathern jars, one full of oil and the rest empty. This they did, and the captain, placing one of his men in each of the empty jars, loaded the asses with them, and

HENLEY

92

drove them into the town to Ali Baba's house. Ali Baba received him hospitably ; and the captain ordered his men, who remained in their jars in the yard, to come out in the middle of the night at a signal from him. He then went to bed ; and Morgiana, happening to need oil, went to help herself out of the jars of the guest : she found, instead of oil, a man in every jar but one. Determined that they should not escape, and heating a quantity of oil, she poured some into each jar, killing the robber within.

So when the captain gave the signal to his men, none of them appeared, and going to the jars, he found them all dead ; so he went his way full of rage and despair, and returned to the cave, and there formed a project of revenge.

Next day he went into the town, and hiring a warehouse, which he furnished with rich goods, became acquainted with Ali Baba's son, who one day

invited him to his father's house. On hearing that the new guest would eat no salt with his meat, Morgiana's suspicions were aroused, and she recognized him as the captain of the robbers.

After dinner she undertook to perform a dance before the company, and at the end of it pointed a dagger at the captain, and then plunged it into his heart. Ali Baba was **very** much shocked, until Morgiana explained the reasons for her conduct; he then gave her to his son in marriage, and they lived in great prosperity and happiness ever after.

THE GIANT HANDS;

OR, THE REWARD OF INDUSTRY.

ONE day at the end of autumn, poor little Willie returned from the forest loaded with as much wood as his feeble strength could bear. He was hungry and tired, for he could scarcely find any wood, so covered was every piece by the fallen leaves. He had also a great sorrow at his heart, for his father had died a few months before, leaving his mother to work hard for the money to support herself and him.

He threw the wood upon the cinders on the hearth, and soon made up a good fire, which threw out a cheerful blaze, at which he warmed his naked, swollen feet, and watched the smoke curling up the wide chimney, and about the rafters of the low roof. He breathed a deep sigh, for he saw no pot on the fire, bubbling up with their frugal dinner; but, alas! they had none, for his poor mother was weak, and could not walk fast to sell the things she had made.

"This must not be any longer," thought he, "for I am getting very big and strong, and have a pair of hands that ought not to be idle. As my mother gets weaker, I should work for her; and as I grow to be a man, she should not work any more, but sit by the fire and get the dinner ready, which I shall then be able to buy for her and me."

Willie was an industrious boy, and did not like to sit idle when his strength—little as it was—might be used to help his dear mother.

So he sat and listened for his mother's footsteps, for he knew she would soon come home, wearied with labour, to share her scanty crust with her boy.

He had not to wait long before the latch lifted and his mother came in. She kissed him, for she loved him much: he was so like his father—the same sort of brow and look of strong will about his face. Again she kissed him, and threw herself into a chair, with tears of fatigue and illness in her eyes.

"Are not you tired, mother dear ? "

"Yes I am, my dear Willie," said she, " and you must be tired too, laddie ; your feet seem quite sore."

"I am a little," said he ; " but I want to tell you what I have on my mind."

He threw his little arms round her neck and kissed her in return, and said,

" I intend to start out into the world and find something to do, that I may no longer be a burden to you. I'll work hard and get money, and you shall have a nice little cottage."

Her heart sank at the idea ; but she saw no other means to save them from being starved, for she was getting weaker every day, and knew not what to do. They talked about this new plan for some hours, till the fire went out, and then they retired to rest.

The morning arose bright and cheerful. The old locker was opened, and his only shoes, taken care of for high days and holidays, were brought out and brushed up, as was also his best suit, which was indeed very little better than the well-worn suit that he wore every day. He, however, thought himself very fine, and felt sure that every one would like him and treat him well.

They sat down to breakfast, but little did they eat, for there was grief in their hearts, and their eyes were moist with tears, which would now and then drop down without their noticing them ; they said nothing, save now and then a few words in a low voice, followed by silence. Willie kept looking at the window, and his mother looked at the fire, for they both felt as if they must cry very much if their looks met.

After some time poor Willie rose and said,

" Well, dear mother, I must be starting."

It was hard work to say this, but he did do it at last, although it was after many struggles to keep down the beatings of his heart.

His mother heard him with a look of surprise and sadness, as if she had not known this before ; and her grief burst forth with wild violence as she threw her arms round his neck with an agony only known to a fond mother.

Willie wept too, but more quietly, and did his best to comfort her, and tried to speak in a hearty cheerful way. Then he put on his hat with a thump, seized his stick and wallet, lifted the latch of the door, opened it wide, took a deep breath of the cool air, and out he went.

Again they lingered in their little garden, where every flower seemed an old friend to be parted with; again the tears and the "Good bye! God bless you!"

At last the little gate was swung wide open, and Willie stepped boldly forth. His mother covered her face and wept. He turned towards her, half inclined, after all, not to go: he felt how difficult it was to leave one so dear; but his duty was simple and he would do it; so with one more "good bye," he was gone on his way, weeping.

The lark rose in the morning sky and sang her joyous song. The sweet fresh air of sunrise cooled his throbbing brow, and his tears ceased to flow; but his little breast heaved now and then with sobs as the storm of grief subsided. His footsteps grew quicker the farther he left his home behind; for before him lay the land of promise, and his little brain was full of dreams of success, and of the joy that would be at his heart when he trod again those fields on his return, laden with riches to throw into his mother's lap.

As these thoughts rushed through his mind, they gave him much comfort; and he even hummed an air as he trotted on, to show his manliness and courage, and flourished his stick about, knocking off with it the twigs on the hedges as he passed them.

He went through a valley that was strewed with sweet wild flowers that bloomed on every side, and stopped to pick some of them, to keep in memory the day when he first went forth to make his fortune.

Just as he was starting again, a curious white cloud appeared across his path, from which came out *two enormous hands.* He started, and well he might, for he saw nobody belonging to them! no, there they were, only hands. There was no fear of them, for they were spread open upon the grass before him as if kindly inviting him to come and meet them.

As he stood gazing with wonder upon them, a voice, which seemed to proceed from the cloud, said,

"Don't be afraid, Willie: I know the good errand that you are on, and I come to be your friend. Persevere in your wish to work, and I will be ever ready to assist you. No eyes but yours will be able to see me, and when you need help you shall have it. Come on, then, and fear not: the road to success is open to you, as it always is to those who do their duty."

"Thank you, good hands," said Willie; "I am sure you mean me good, for I am too little for you to wish to harm."

The hands vanished, and Willie went on his way.

All his grief went at once: he saw quite plainly the way to success; shouted some loud huzzas, jumped from the path into the road, and from the road into the path again; then set off running and leaping, wild with joy.

"Nothing can stop me now," said he, "hurrah!"

However, as the day grew on, he went along more steadily, for he was not used to so much walking and running, and therefore began to get tired; so at last he threw himself upon the grass, and looked upwards to the blue sky, and watched the light clouds pursue each other across the boundless heavens, and admired the many strange shapes the clouds had. One cloud looked just like

his mother's cottage, with the smoke coming out of the chimney, and he thought how lonely she must be by herself; another cloud was like a purse full of money, and another was a waggon full of furniture and Christmas cheer.

"Ah!" thought he, "before long there shall be a real purse for my mother, and a real waggon with wooden furniture in it, and all for her."

As he lay, half dreaming, he thought he heard something like the rolling of thunder; he listened and listened until he was sure there was something near at hand that caused these curious sounds. He rose and went where the sounds seemed to come from, which grew louder and louder as he went on, until he came to the edge of a precipice, and saw a grand and awful rush of foaming waters, which threw themselves headlong down between the rocks with a deafening roar.

He looked from right to left, and he could not see any way of crossing. All his gaiety left him, as he saw it was not possible for him to proceed. After standing some time near the edge of the cataract, thinking now that all his hopes were gone, he sat himself down and wept.

He had not been many minutes in his grief when he felt himself gently lifted from the ground by a gigantic hand, which passed him high above the waters, and placed him in safety on the opposite bank. As the hand put him on his feet, it became so much like a cloud that he could scarcely see it ; but before it had quite vanished, Willie took off his hat, and bowing, said,

"Thank you kindly, good hand. You have kept your promise well."

Certain now that the fairy hands were not a dream, which he had really begun to think them, his courage and hope became strong again, and his heart was light and gay, for he knew there was a strong power watching over him and ready to help him.

He soon came to a dense wood, where the giant trees twisted their thick limbs round each other in the oddest ways, and the briers and shrubs on the ground twined their long branches together, as if they were serpents, and right across they made a barrier that only a strong brave foot could get through. But Willie looked upon all such obstacles as nothing compared with the last which the fairy hands lifted him over. So at it he went, striking right and left with his good stick to clear his way.

As he was laying about with a right good will, he was brought to a standstill by a ferocious growl. He turned his eyes around, and beheld, much to his dismay, a fierce wolf preparing to spring upon him. He shrank down with terror as he looked upon the white teeth and fiery eyes of the savage brute, and gave himself up for lost, when, to his joy, one of the great hands appeared from amidst the thick foliage of a tree, and placed itself between him and his enemy ; at the same time the other hand seized the wolf, and crushed it in its grasp.

Willie fell on his knees, and returned thanks for his safety ; then, looking round for the hands, he found they had vanished.

Wearied with his journey, he sat down under a tree, thinking he would rest for the night ; and pulling out his wallet, began to

eat some of the bread and cheese that his kind mother had put
in it : he had scarcely eaten any all day, for his mind had been
so full of thoughts about the wonderful appearance of the good
hands, that he had quite forgotten to have his dinner.

After finishing his meal, which he did with very great relish, he
began to turn over in his mind how he was to make up his bed in
his very large bed-chamber, for it appeared as if he had got the
great forest all to himself. When he had got together enough dried
leaves to make his resting-place softer, he prepared to lie down,
when, to his very great delight, he beheld the gigantic hands spread
themselves over him, with the fingers entwined, making for him the

most perfect little tent in the world. How his heart bounded with gratitude towards the good fairy hands, as he felt how safely he might sleep beneath them!

"Thank you again, good hands," said he, "for your kind care of me; but, before I say my prayers, cannot you, since you are so powerful, tell me something of my dear mother—whether she is more happy, and whether she has food to eat?"

"Good Willie," replied a voice, "your mother knows that you will be protected, as all good children are; and she has food, for she is industrious: her hands were given to her from my kingdom, in which no idle hands are ever made, as you shall know from me hereafter.

Sleep, then, in peace, that you may rise prepared for labour on the coming morn."

So Willie slept.

Willie was early afoot, for he believed what the voice had told him, that the day was to be a day of labour, with some good luck at the end of it. He soon got through the wood, and left it behind him, and saw a huge castle a little way off.

"Here, surely, is something to be done," thought he; so he leapt up the steps, and tried to raise the knocker, but it was too heavy for his strength. In an instant the hands appeared, and grasped the knocker, and gave such a rat-tat-tat that it sounded like thunder through the valley, and you might have heard it rumbling away on the distant mountains.

The door opened with a sudden jerk, and in the porch stood the mistress of the mansion, scowling like a bear. The moment Willie saw her, he went backward down the steps, for she was an ogress, and as ugly as all ogresses are. She glared upon the little man, whom she supposed had given that great knock, with surprise and anger ; and then, in a voice like a very hoarse raven, she cried,

" How dared you knock like that at my door, you little varlet? You have put me all in a twitter."

Willie trembled, took off his hat, and replied in an humble voice, " If you please, Princess, I wished to know whether you wanted a servant to assist in your fine castle."

" A servant, brat ! " she said ; " what can you do ? "

" Anything to please your Highness, for I want to work."

" Oh, oh ! do you ? Then come in, for my servants have all left me because I don't put my work out," said she.

With that, Willie entered, and soon found that he had plenty to do ; for his first job was to get the ogress's dinner ready, who, in truth, had a wonderful appetite, for there were many sorts of provisions—fish, fowl, beef, soup, mutton, and hampers of vegetables.

He sighed as he looked upon such abundance, which would have been dinner enough for all the people in his native village. Again he sighed ; as he did so, the giant hands appeared. If you could only have seen them truss this, skewer that, boil the other, turn out the sauces, pick the pickles, cut the bread, and put the dishes to the fire, you would have wondered—Willie himself doing all he could to aid in the work.

The ogress dined, and said nothing for the first hour, eating as fast as she could ; but when she had finished the last round of beef, she smiled upon her treasure of a servant, and said he was a better cook than all her servants put together.

Selfish people are always ungrateful; and so the ogress was, for she wanted poor Willie to do more and more, cooking dinners and suppers, so that he had not a minute's rest; and, one day, when she had been requiring more than usual, he turned round and told her that she left him hardly time to sleep, and that her appetite was frightful.

Could you have seen her face, you would have been as frightened as Willie was.

" Little wretch ! " screamed she, " I have half a mind to snap you up as I would the wing of a chicken ; and, remember from this

moment, if my dinner is short of what I want, I will eat you to make up for what you have left undone."

"Then I shall leave you," said Willie.

Rage made the face of the ogress glow like a furnace as she made a pounce at poor Willie for his angry speech; and she would have caught him in her gripe had he not dodged round a large bundle of vegetables which luckily lay on the floor. Round and round she went after him, until he felt that he must be caught— when a very large hand grasped her round the waist, and hurried her, yelling, out of the kitchen: Willie following, returning thanks for his escape. They came to a large window which opened to the

sea; the hand thrust the ogress out, and right above the rolling
waves it held her, while the sea-birds flew round about, with shrill
cries, in terror at a sight so strange.

"Mercy! mercy!" the ogress cried out, as she looked upon the
awful depth beneath her.

The hand let go its hold; and the ogress, with a dreadful scream,
whirled over and over, and fell with such a plump into the sea, that
the spray flew over the highest tower, and the fishes swam away in
terror. She went down, down, down; but never came up, up, up.

Willie ran out of the front door, and when he got to the margin
of the sea, he looked back at the huge castle, and saw the giant

hands at work destroying it. Down came the big stones; smash
went the strong rafters; the dust flew up in thick clouds; and in a
few minutes the ogress's castle was a heap of ruins. He turned his
eye to the waves, expecting every moment to see the head of the
ogress pop up again; but it did not. He saw the good hands following him: they plunged into the sea close at his feet; he jumped
into the palm of one, and seated himself. Between the finger and
thumb of each hand was one of his cooking forks, stuck through
two of the ogress's best handkerchiefs, which made very capital sails,
catching the wind and wafting him along over the sea just as well
as the last invention in boats.

As the moon rose, it found him safely landed and snug under the roof of a good farmer who had promised him work—ay, even as much as he could do; but the farmer did not know what a treasure he had in Willie, for the next morning he was working in his shirt-sleeves in the corn-field, reaping and sheaving, and doing as much work as two stout men could do. But there, under the shelter of the high corn, were the friendly hands working miracles—gathering up the corn, and putting it into sheaves in a manner that could not be done by mortal hands.

Willie whistled, and cut away, caring nothing for the burning heat of the sun: his sickle glistened, and the corn fell in such long

sweeps that I do believe it was as wonderful as the hands themselves.

The longest day will, however, have an end, and so did this. It
had been a long day of hard work, lasting from the rise of sun till
twilight; but when Willie's first day waned, then came out the farmer, bringing with him his daughter, to enjoy a walk in the cool of
the day. The farmer stared when he looked upon the golden rows
of heavy corn standing for his admiration in the well-tied sheaves.
He looked from the little man to the fruits of his labour, and promised to himself to do his best to keep so good a servant; his
daughter also, a beautiful girl, glanced an admiring look at the

glowing face of Willie, as he stood with sickle in one hand and cap in the other.

"Oh, oh!" said the farmer, "if he can reap so well, perhaps he can plough."

So the next morning found little Willie as a ploughman.

But how could he know how to do it? any one would say. Why, the hands guided the plough; and the land was ploughed in furrows as straight as the flight of an arrow.

The farmer watched from his window, but the hands he could not see; he saw the plough cut its way into the earth, without going a single inch out of its proper track, and in a manner that surprised him, and he again blessed his good fortune that had given him such a wonderful labourer.

Willie sat at the board of the good farmer, who thought he could not make too much of him, for he was grateful to the industrious youth, who seemed to take pleasure in working for his master.

Time rolled on, and Willie became quite head man, for it was found that he could be trusted with anything. One day, when he was out on the mountains, where he had gone to gather the flocks for the shearing, heavy storms came on, and the floods deluged the valley, sweeping away, in their headlong course, the flocks and herds of other farmers. Willie wisely kept his master's flock upon the mountain's side until the rain was nearly over; but when he came down into the valleys, he was alarmed to find that, in many places, the brooks had swollen into rivers, too wide and deep for his sheep to pass over. By the side of the first of these rivers he stood in deep thought.

"How shall I get across? I wish the hands would help me now!"

In a moment the giant hands spread themselves over the turbid waters, forming a most perfect bridge. He drove the sheep across without fear, and reached his master's house in safety, much to the joy of all, who had given him up for lost.

Willie lay down that night full of gratitude for his great good fortune, and thought of his home, to which he knew he should soon return to take happiness to his fond mother. He was nearly asleep, and thoughts were getting mixed with dreams, when a loud shout of "Fire! Fire!" roused him up again with a startling shock. Up he rose, and dressed quickly, the cries waxing louder and louder. He ran down the stairs, the smoke nearly choking him, for the HOUSE WAS ON FIRE! rushed into the farmyard, there he saw his master, with the servants, running about frantic with fright; no

water handy, no fire-engines, everybody shouting, pigs squealing, and the geese cackling. The flames made their way from room to room, and reached the chamber of the farmer's daughter. What can be done now? The staircase has been burnt, no ladder can reach the window; there stands the girl, the smoke all about her; very soon it will be too late!

Willie looked on in despair, for he could devise no means to save the poor child; when suddenly the giant hands appeared, and placing themselves against the side of the house, formed a ladder, up which Willie quickly sprang. In a few moments he reached the window, and folding the girl in his arms, rushed down the friendly

hands, and placed her, safe and sound, in the embrace of her weeping
father.

*   *   *   *   *   *   *

A heavily-laden waggon creaks along the winding road, covered
with a tilt as white as snow; but what has it inside? You can peep
and see. Beautiful tables and chairs, and sides of bacon, and geese
and chickens, and fair round cheeses, and rolls of golden butter, with
white eggs peeping through the bars of the wicker baskets. Where
is the waggon going? To market, perhaps. Ask the youth who
is trudging by its side, with a smiling, happy face, ruddy with health
and the warm tinge of the sun.

Why, I declare that it is Willie, grown quite stout and strong!
Where is he going with that well-stored waggon, which really has
no horses to draw it, and yet it goes forward at a pretty pace? Why,
I do believe the giant hands are dragging it along!

It is Willie, indeed; and, joyous moment! he is going home.
In his pocket he has much bright silver, the produce of his labour.
The good things in the waggon were given to him by the farmer
to show his gratitude to Willie for being so useful and active, and,
more than all, for saving his darling child from perishing in the
flames.

At last the cottage path is reached. His mother is standing at the gate. Willie shouts—such a hearty shout! His mother looks upon him, but cannot speak : he is soon in her arms.

That night they sat late beside their blazing hearth. Amidst the smoke might now be seen a large well-filled pot bubbling with something more than water in it. How much Willie had to tell his mother of his labour, and what he owed to the wonderful giant hands, for saving him from harm in every danger, and for helping him whenever he needed help! Willie's mother smiled upon him when he came to the end of his story, and gave him many a kiss.

"Dear child," said she, "you have been indeed fortunate; but you deserved it. That which appears to you as a miracle is none. Those giant hands have been known to many, and their power is very great; they always assist the willing and the good; the reward they bestow is certain; they are the powerful *hands of Industry*."

Willie stayed now with his mother, and the two managed a nice little farm, which became in a few years a large one. He then went to see the good farmer, and to see the farmer's daughter too, who had admired him when he was reaping, and whom he saved from the fire.

Soon after, Willie and Nelly, for that was her name, were married, and they lived many happy years. Willie became a rich farmer, and taught his neighbours "how to farm profitably," and the way was this :

Be Honest, and Industrious, and Kind, and the Giant Hands will be sure to help you.

GOODY TWO-SHOES.

IN the latter part of the reign of Queen Bess there was an honest industrious countryman named Meanwell, living upon a small farm which he held under Sir Peter Gripe, a very hard, covetous landlord, who was persuaded by one of his richer tenants, Hugh Graspall, as greedy as himself, to take away the lands held by Meanwell and other poor tenants, and let him have them to increase his own large farm.

When Meanwell was thus cruelly turned out of his little farm, which had enabled him to support a wife and two young children called Tommy and Margery, he tried in vain to find another cottage with land. Care and misfortune soon shortened his days; and his wife, not long after, followed him to the grave. On her death-bed she did not repine at her losses and sufferings, but humbly prayed that Heaven would watch over and protect her helpless orphans when she should be taken from them. At her death these poor children were left in a sad plight; and as there were but few people in the village of Mouldwell, where they lived, able to befriend them, they could get no regular meals, and had to make all sorts of shifts to keep themselves from starving. At times, indeed, they were obliged to put up with the wild fruits and berries that they picked from the hedges. They were also without proper clothes to keep them warm; and as for shoes, they had not even two pairs between them. Tommy, who had to go about more than his sister, had a pair to himself; but little Margery for a long time wore but one shoe.

These two children in all their trials never ceased to love each other dearly, nor did they forget the good lessons which their kind mother had taught them. And well did they deserve her anxious love, and the earnest prayers she had offered up to Heaven for their welfare. They never murmured, nor ever thought of taking anything from their neighbours, however hungry they might be, but were always looking out for some sort of work, although but little of that did they get. But this hard lot really befell them for their good; for, without it, how could their excellent qualities have been so well brought out, and their praiseworthy conduct have become the talk of the village?

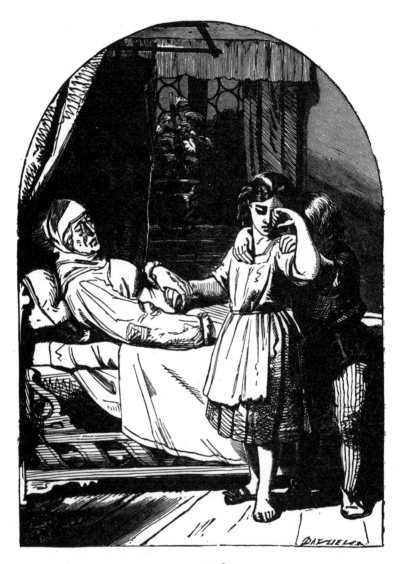

THE DYING MOTHER'S BLESSING.

118

Heaven, indeed, had heard their dying mother's prayers, and had watched over and protected them through all their troubles. Relief was at hand, and better things were in store for them. It happened that Mr. Goodall, the worthy clergyman of the parish, heard of their sad wandering sort of life—for they were without a home, and had generally to sleep in some barn or outhouse—and so he sent for the two children, and kindly offered to shelter them until they could get regular work to do. Immediately after this unlooked-for blessing had fallen upon them, a gentleman of rank and wealth came from London on a visit at the parsonage; and no sooner did he hear the story of the orphans, than his heart warmed towards them, and he resolved to be their friend.

The very first thing he did was to order a pair of shoes to be made for Margery, and he also placed money in her hand to buy good and suitable clothes with. But he did much more than this for Tommy. Not only did he get clothes for him, but he offered to take him to London if he would consent to go, promising to put him in a way to do well by going abroad, after he had acquired sufficient knowledge to fit him for such a step.

When the time arrived for her brother to start off with his generous friend, Margery was in great trouble, and her eyes filling with tears, they embraced each other over and over again; but Tommy, in order to comfort his weeping sister, promised he would not fail to come over to Mouldwell to see her, when he should return from foreign countries.

After he was gone Margery began to recover her usual cheerfulness. She knew it was of no use to keep on crying; but what helped greatly to put her into good spirits was the pleasure she took in her new shoes. As soon as the old shoemaker brought them she put them on, and ran at once to the clergyman's wife, crying out with glee, as she pointed to them,

"Two shoes, ma'am! See, two shoes!"

These words, "two shoes!" she kept on repeating to everybody she met, and by this means came to be called for a long while after by the name of GOODY TWO-SHOES.

Now, Margery was a thoughtful little girl; and after she had lived at the parsonage some time, she noticed more and more how good and wise the clergyman was, and she could only suppose that this was owing to his great learning. The poor girl then felt ashamed of her own ignorance, and was most anxious to learn how to read and write, although at that time in distant country places very little instruction was given to poor children. Mr. Goodall, however, when he found how desirous she was to improve herself in every way, kindly taught her what she most wished to know. As he was a clever man, he took care that she should not learn by rote; so, as she advanced, he made her think well over each lesson, and though this made her progress a little slower, she became in good time a better scholar than any of the children who went to the village school. As soon as she found that this was the case, she began to reflect that it was her duty to devote some of her spare time, with Mr. Goodall's permission, to the instruction of such poor children as could not go to school. After much thinking and contriving, she hit upon a simple but clever plan to get these ignorant children to attend to her teaching. She knew that the different letters of the alphabet were sufficient to spell every word—only that those used as capital letters were larger than the others. Now as very few books were then printed, and they were scarcely ever to be seen in the hands of poor people, she thought she could get over the difficulty by cutting, with a good knife, out of several pieces of wood, six sets of capital letters like these—

A B C D E F G H I J K L M N O P Q R S T U V W X Y Z.

And ten sets of these common letters—

a b c d e f g h i j k l m n o p q r s t u v w x y z.

When, after much pains and trouble, she had finished all these wooden letters, she managed with some difficulty to borrow an old spelling-book, and, with the help of this, she made her playmates set up the words she wished them to spell. Her usual way with them, when she could get several of them together about her, was this: Suppose the word to be spelt was "Pudding" (she always chose words at first that sounded pleasantly to her little pupils' ears), one of the children, who were placed in a circle round her, brought the capital letter "P" from the large set; the next picked up "u" from the small set; the next two a "d" each; the next "i," and so on, until the whole word was spelt. Margery, in her simplicity, fancied that the first steps in knowledge ought to be as much *like play as possible;* and the result proved how right she was, for her little companions were always eager for this "game," as they called it, and were very sorry if they were thrown out by picking up a wrong letter, and had to play no more that morning. Before long, not only her poor pupils, but their ignorant parents too, were very thankful for the trouble she took in teaching her playfellows; and as it often happened they could not be spared to be with her of a morning, she would then go round to their different cottages to teach them, carrying her wooden letters in a basket. .

On one of these occasions the worthy clergyman asked a friend of his, a substantial yeoman named Rowland, to accompany Margery in her rounds, that he might judge as an eye-witness of the results of her teaching. This good man was much pleased with all he saw and heard ; and, as he gave his opinion in writing to Mr. Goodall, we cannot do better than make use of his own words.

"After setting out, Margery and I, we first came to Jerry Hodge's ; and no sooner had we tapped at the door than the cottager's wife came out, and when she saw Margery, said, 'Oh, if it isn't little Goody Two-Shoes; and I am right glad to see thee, that I be! Pray come in, and this good gentleman too, that ye may both see how well our Billy has learned his lessons.' The poor little fellow, I found, could not speak plain ; but he had learned all his letters, and was quite able to pick them out, and put them together in short words, when asked to do so.

"The next place we visited was Widow Giles's, who, to protect herself at night, kept a fierce-looking dog, and the moment Margery

opened the gate he began barking at a great rate.   This called out
his mistress, who scolded him sharply for daring to bark at Goody
Two-Shoes. After quieting the noisy cur, she asked us in, and seemed
very proud to show how clever her little Sally was in learning her
lessons ; indeed, I found the child was very ready at spelling, and
she pronounced the words clearly and correctly also.

   "We then called at Toby Cook's cottage.   Here a number of
children were met together to play, who all came round Margery
very fondly, and begged her to 'set the game' for them.   She then

took out her wooden letters from her basket, and asked the girl who was next to her what she was to have for dinner. 'Apple pie,' she answered, and went to look for a capital 'A'; the next two produced a 'p' each, and so they went on until they had spelt 'Apple pie' complete. Other words were given by the children, chiefly the names of things they liked and were used to, such as bread, milk, beef, &c., which were for the most part spelt carefully, very few mistakes having been made, until the game was finished. After this, she set them the following lesson to get by heart—

'He that will thrive Must rise by five.'	'Tell me with whom you go, And I'll tell what you do.'
'He that has thriven May lie till seven.'	'A friend in need Is a friend indeed.'
'Truth may be blamed, But cannot be shamed.'	'Love your friends who are true, And your friends will love you.'

"Margery next took me to see Kitty Sullen. This little girl used to be very self-willed and vain, because she could dress more finely than the poor cottagers' children. I was glad to see, however, that she paid attention to Margery's good advice; and I hear it generally reported that Madge has done wonders by setting her an example of humility and kindness, and that she has much softened her stubborn heart.

"On our way homeward we saw a well-dressed gentleman sitting under a couple of great trees, at the corner of the rookery. He had a sort of crutch by him, and seemed to be ailing. But perhaps this was partly put on, that he might try Margery's wit; for as soon as he saw us he called out to her to come near him, and then said, more in jest than in pain, 'Pray, little maid, can you tell me what I must do to get well?' 'Yes, good sir,' she replied readily: 'go to bed when the rooks do, and get up with them at morn; earn, as they do, what you eat; and then you will get health and keep it.' The gentleman seemed quite taken with the good sense of her reply, and with her modest look too, and begged her to accept a small silver coin as a token of his regard for her merit."

One day, as Margery was coming home from the next village, she met with some wicked, idle boys, who had tied a young raven to a staff, and were just about to make a victim of the poor thing by throwing stones at it. She offered at once to buy the raven for a penny, and this they agreed to. She then brought him home to the parsonage, and gave him the name of Ralph, and a fine bird he

was.   Madge soon taught him to speak several words, **and also to**
pick up letters, and even to spell a word or two.

Some years before Margaret began to teach the poor cottagers'
children, Sir Walter Welldon, a wealthy knight, living in the neighbourhood, had set up an elderly widow lady, who had seen better
days, in a small school in the village of Mouldwell, that she might
teach the children of those who could afford to pay something towards it.   This gentlewoman, whose name was Gray, was at length
taken seriously ill, and was no longer able to attend to her duties.
When Sir Walter heard of this, he sent for Mr. Goodall, and asked

him to look out for some one who would be able and willing to take Mrs. Gray's place as mistress of the school.

The worthy clergyman could not think of one so well qualified for the task as Margery Meanwell, who, though but young, was grave beyond her years, and was growing up to be a comely maiden; and when he told his mind to the knight, Margery was chosen by the latter at once as the successor of poor Mrs. Gray. Sir Walter continued to be very good to the sick widow until she died, which

happened shortly afterwards. He likewise built a larger school-house for Margery's use. This she needed, for she would have all her old pupils without payment about her that liked to come to the school, as well as the regular scholars belonging to it.

From this time no one called her "Goody Two-Shoes," but generally Mrs. Margery, and she was more and more liked and respected by her neighbours.

Soon after Mrs. Margery had become mistress of the school, she was lucky enough to save a dove from the hands of some cruel boys, who were tormenting the poor creature, and she called him Tom, in remembrance of her brother now far away, and from whom she had heard no tidings ever since he left her. But in those bygone days writing letters was not much practised, and there was no such thing as a post-office to be seen anywhere. Tom learned to pick up a few letters, but he was not so clever as her old favourite Ralph, and of course could not be taught to utter a single word.

About this time a lamb had lost its dam, and its owner was about to have it killed. When Mrs. Margery heard of this, she bought the gentle creature of him and brought it home, thinking to please and benefit her pupils by putting such an example before them of going early to bed. Some neighbours, finding how fond of such pets Mrs. Margery was, presented her with a nice playful little dog called Jumper, and also with a skylark. Now Master Ralph was a shrewd bird, and a bit of a wag too; and when Will the lamb, and Carol the lark, made their appearance, the knowing fellow picked out the following verse, to the great amusement of everybody—

> "Early to bed, and early to rise,
> Is the way to be healthy, wealthy, and wise."

Mrs. Margery was ever on the look-out to be useful to her neighbours. Knowing more than they did, she was often able to give them good advice, and to save them from losses which they were about to incur through their ignorance. Many of these good folks depended much on their hay. Now a traveller coming from London had presented Mrs. Margery with a new kind of instrument, a rough-looking barometer, very inferior to those now used, by the help of which she could often guess correctly how the weather would be a day or two beforehand. She made herself so useful, indeed, that they all came to her for advice, and profited by it in often getting in their hay without damage, while much of that in the neighbouring villages was spoiled. This caused a great talk about the country; and so provoked were the people of the distant villages at the better luck of the Mouldwell folks, that they accused Mrs. Margery of being a witch, and sent old Nicky Noodle, a numskull and a gossiping busybody, to go and tax her with it, and to scrape together whatever evidence he could against her. When this wiseacre saw her at her school door, with her raven on one shoulder and the dove on the other, the lark on her hand, and the lamb and little dog by her side, the sight took his breath away for a time, and he scampered off crying out, "A witch! a witch! a witch!"

She laughed at the simpleton's folly, and called him jocosely a "conjuror" for his pains; but poor Mrs. Margery did not know how much folly and wickedness there was in the world, and she was

greatly surprised to find that the half-witted Nicky Noodle had got a warrant against her.

At the meeting of the justices, before whom she was summoned to appear, many of her neighbours were present, ready to speak up for her character, if needful. But it turned out that the charge made against her was nothing more than Nicky's idle tale that she was a witch. Now-a-days, it seems strange that such a thing could be; but in England, at that period, so fondly styled by some "the good old times," many silly and wicked things were constantly being done, especially by the rich and powerful, against the poor— such things as would not now be borne. Amongst such old blind follies was a common belief in witchcraft, the practice of which was severely punishable by law; and many a poor harmless old woman, against whom her ignorant neighbours had a spite, has been tortured even to death, on the stupid charge of being a witch.

It happened that among the justices who met to hear this charge against Mrs. Margery, there was but one silly enough to think there was any ground for it. His name was Shallow, and it was he who had granted the warrant. But she soon silenced him when he kept repeating that she *must* be a witch to foretell the weather, besides harbouring many strange creatures about her. After pointing to the friends who had come to speak for her character and her truth, she said very calmly, looking at this weak man full in the face,

" I never supposed that any one here could be so weak as to believe that there was any such thing as a witch. But if I am a witch, here is my charm," she added, laying her weather-glass upon the table; " this it is alone that has helped me to know the state of the weather. And as for my animal companions, your worship even might profit as I have done by their good example. My tender dove," she continued, " is a pattern of true love; my watchful raven of forethought ; my joyous lark of thankfulness ; my gentle lamb of innocence ; and my trusty dog of sagacity. If it be witchcraft to have such teachers to remind me of my duties, then, indeed, am I witch, please your worship—at your service."

Fortunately her patron, Sir Walter Welldon, one of the justices present, was well acquainted with the use of the new instrument. When he had explained its nature to his foolish brother justice, he turned the whole charge into ridicule, and finished by giving Mrs. Margery such a high character for knowledge, prudence, and charity, that the bench of justices not only released her at once from the trumpery charge, but gave her their public thanks for the good services she had done in their neighbourhood.

One of these gentlemen, Sir Edward Lovell, an intimate friend of Sir Walter's, conceived, indeed, so high an opinion of her virtues and abilities, that, having been lately left a widower, he offered her very liberal terms if she would consent to come to his house, take the management of it, and educate his daughter also. She respectfully declined this handsome offer, for she thought it was her duty to continue teaching the children of the poor, who, but for her, she feared, would remain in ignorance.

Several months after this Sir Edward fell ill, and was for some time in a state of danger. He then repeated his request that Mrs. Margery would come to take charge of his house, now that he was quite unable to manage it, and look after his dear children. The thoughtful young woman then took counsel with her kind old friend the clergyman, and by his advice she agreed to undertake the proposed employment until Sir Edward's restoration to health. She completely won that gentleman's respect and admiration by her skill and tenderness in nursing him during the remainder of his illness, and by the great care she took of his children. All the members of his household loved her for her goodness.

By the time that Sir Edward fully regained his health, he had

become more and more attached to Mrs. Margery. He thought she could hardly be matched for propriety of conduct, for good sense, and for sweetness of temper; and with all this he fancied, too, that she had not her equal anywhere for good looks. It was not, then, to be wondered at that when she talked of going back to her school, he should feel dull and melancholy, nor that, after due reflection, he should offer her his hand in marriage. We know already how modest and free from vanity and false pride Mrs. Margery was. This proposal, therefore, took her quite by surprise, and so undeserving did she think herself of the honour intended her, that at first she was inclined not to accept it, but this her rich suitor would not hear of; and as her true friends, Sir Walter and Mr. Goodall, tried hard to persuade her to accept Sir Edward's hand, telling her she would then be enabled to do many more good works than she had ever done before, she at last yielded. She had not at all objected because she did not like Sir Edward, for she really loved and admired him as he deserved, but only because she feared it was not her duty to leave her old humble friends to be a fine lady.

All things having been settled, and the day fixed, the great folks and others in the neighbourhood came in crowds to see the wedding; for glad they were that one who had, ever since she was a child, been so deserving, was to be thus rewarded. Just as the bride and bridegroom were about to enter the church, their friends assembled outside were busily engaged in watching the progress of a horseman handsomely dressed and mounted, and as gay in appearance as a courtier, who was galloping up a distant slope leading to the church, as eagerly as if he wanted to get there before the marriage should take place. When all was in readiness for the holy ceremony to commence, and the clergyman just going to open his book, a strange gentleman, richly dressed, no other, indeed, than the horseman who had been before noticed by the crowd, rushed into the church, calling out that they should stop the marriage. All were astonished at this interruption, particularly the couple about to be united, each of whom the stranger immediately addressed apart. During this parley, the bystanders were more and more surprised, especially when they saw Sir Edward standing almost speechless, and his bride crying and fainting away in the stranger's arms. But this seeming grief was soon over, and was presently converted into a flood of joy. This gentleman, so elegantly dressed, proved to be no other than Margery's brother, our former acquaintance little Tommy, now Mr. Meanwell, just returned with great honour and profit from a distant foreign country. As soon as the news reached him that his sister was going to be married, he resolved to take horse from London, where he then was, and try to reach the spot in time to find out whether it was a suitable match for one so dear to him as Margery was, and to whom he was now able to give a fortune if she needed it. All was soon explained, and the loving couple then returned to the altar, and were married, to the satisfaction of all present.

After her happy marriage, Lady Lovell continued to practise all

kinds of good. She was not content in giving largely in the way
of charity, but she constantly went about visiting the poor, cheering
them up and helping them in their troubles, and comforting them
in sickness. She took great pains in increasing and improving the
school of which she had been the mistress, and placed there a poor
but worthy scholar and his wife to preside over it. She lived
happily with Sir Edward for many years; and as her life had been
regarded as the greatest blessing, so her death was looked upon
as the greatest calamity that had befallen the neighbourhood for
many years.

JACK AND THE BEANSTALK.

—o—

An idle, careless boy was Jack, and though his father was dead, and his mother was very poor, he did not like to work, so at last they had no money left to buy bread; they had nothing but the cow. Then Jack's mother sent him to the market to sell the cow. But as he went he met a man who had some pretty beans in his hand, which he stopped to look at.

The man said, " Give me the ugly white cow, and you shall have the beans."

" Thank you, sir," said Jack, and ran home to show his mother how well he had sold the cow. She was very angry, and threw the beans into the garden, and sat down to cry, for she had no fire nor bread.

133

Jack had to go to bed without supper; he woke late next morning, and thought his window was dark, and when he looked out, he saw that all the beans had taken root in the garden, and had grown up and twisted like a ladder, which seemed to reach to the sky. Jack ran down to the garden, and began to climb, though his mother cried out to him to stop, and threw her shoes at him. He did not mind her at all, but went on and on, above the houses, above the trees, above the steeples, till he came to a strange land. Then he got off the beanstalk, to try and find a house where he might beg a piece of bread.

As he was looking round, he saw an old Fairy leaning on a staff, who told him he must go straight on till he came to a large house, where a fierce giant lived. She said this giant had killed Jack's father, and kept all his money, and that Jack must be very brave, and must kill the wicked giant, and get all the money back for his poor mother. Jack thought it would be hard to kill a giant, but he would try, so he went on till he met the giant's wife. He asked

for a bit of bread, and she gave him some, for she was not a bad woman, and when she heard the giant coming, she hid Jack in the oven for fear the giant should eat him.

The giant was very cross; he wanted his supper, and said he smelt fresh meat; but his wife said he smelt the people who were shut up in the cellar to fatten.

After he had eaten as much supper as would have served ten men, he called for his hen. Then a pretty little hen stepped out of a basket, and every time the giant said "Lay," it laid a golden egg.

Jack thought this hen must have been his father's, and when the giant was tired of seeing the hen lay golden eggs, and fell asleep, he stole out of the oven, took up the hen, and ran as fast as he could to the beanstalk. You may be sure he made haste to slide down, and very glad his mother was to see him and the hen. Then they sold the golden eggs, and bought many nice things with the money.

But Jack said he must kill the giant; so he

stained his face with walnut-juice, and put on other clothes, and set out up the beanstalk again. He went to beg of the giant's wife, but she was a long time before she would let him in. At last she took him to the kitchen, gave him some plum tart and milk, and let him sleep in a closet where the pans were kept.

When the giant came in, he said he smelt fresh meat; but his wife said it was only a dead horse, and she gave him a large loaf and a whole cheese and a pailful of beer for his supper. When he had done, he took out his money-bags, and counted his money till he fell asleep. Then Jack came out on tiptoe, lifted up the heavy bags, and made haste to the beanstalk, where he was glad to let the bags slide down first, and then to slide after them.

Now they were rich, for it was their own money, and Jack's mother lived like a lady.

Still Jack did not forget what the Fairy had told him to do, so he climbed up the beanstalk once more, and went on to the house of the giant. But

he tried a long time before the old woman would let him in, for she said her husband had been robbed by beggar-boys. But in the end she gave him a cake, and before the giant came in, hid him in a copper, and set a round of beef on the table to stop her husband from looking for fresh meat. He ate all the beef and drank so much rum that he could not stand, but lay back, and called for his harp. His wife brought the harp, which was silver, with golden strings, and when the giant said " Play," it played the sweetest music you ever heard.

Then Jack said, " I will have the harp," and as soon as the giant began to snore, he took up the harp, and ran off.

But the harp was a Fairy, and it called out " Master! Master!" till the giant awoke, and ran after the boy ; but for all his long strides, he was so drunk that Jack got to the beanstalk first, and you may be sure he was not long in coming down.

Then the giant began to come down after him, and when Jack's mother saw the wicked wretch, she

cried out for fear; but Jack said, "Never fear, mother, but bring me an axe."

His mother made great haste to bring him an axe; then Jack, who was now grown a stout lad, began to hew down the beanstalk.

When the last beanstalk was cut through, Jack and his mother ran a good way off, and they saw the giant fall from a great height to the ground, which shook with his weight, and when they went up they found he was quite dead. Then the good Fairy came and touched the beanstalk with her staff, and it was carried away by the wind, which Jack's mother was very glad of. Then she gave them all their riches that the giant had stolen, but Jack gave the giant's kind wife as much as she liked, and he grew up after to be a very good boy, and was never more idle or careless.

JACK THE GIANT-KILLER.

————o————

In ancient times the good people of Cornwall were sadly frightened at many wicked giants, who came from different places, robbing and killing all that fell in their way. Amongst them was the giant Cormoran, who had a great castle on a rock which stood in the sea. He often waded through the water and came over to the coast, when all the people would flee before him. After he had feasted himself upon their cattle, he would carry off with him a number of sheep and oxen, slung across his back.

Now, there was a very little fellow, named Jack, who was not like other boys, but was as bold and as strong as a man; and when he was told the shocking things that had been done by Cormoran, he would say to his father quite bravely, "Shouldn't I like to kill that giant!"

One night, having heard from his father more sad tales of Cormoran's doings, Jack felt more than ever a wish to kill him; so by-and-bye he slipped out, and got together a dark lantern, a pickaxe, a shovel, and a horn, and with these he left the house quietly, and came near the giant's castle, which stood on a hill.

Jack then dug a huge pit, just at the foot of the hill, over which he strewed sticks and turf, so that it looked like the rest of the ground. At daylight he went to the castle gate, and blew his horn so loudly that he aroused the giant, who roared out,

"You little villain! you shall pay dearly for this!"

Down the hill he rushed after Jack, until he came to the bottom, and in a moment tumbled head-over-heels into the pit. There he stuck fast, Jack all the while crowing over him, and asking why he did not come out and meet him like a man. Jack then laid hold of his pickaxe, and taking a good aim, struck Cormoran a terrible blow on the crown of his head, which killed him outright.

One day, when Jack was strolling about, a giant pounced upon him, carried him home in his pocket, and threw him into a room full of bones, telling him to be quiet while he sharpened a knife to kill him with, for he meant to cook him for dinner, if he could get another giant who lived close by to come and dine with him. Jack looked about the room, and found two strong ropes; he made loops at one end of each, got up to the window, and waited till the two giants came to the door. Directly they were under the window, he dropped a loop over each head, and quickly threw the ends over a beam, and hoisted them from the ground, kicking and struggling. Jack then glided down the ropes, and put an

end to the giants with his new sharp sword, and let all the prisoners loose.

Jack next came to a great house, and a giant with two heads asked him to walk in. After supper, he put him in the best bed; but Jack, fearing mischief, kept wide awake. Presently the giant crept softly up to the bed, and banged away upon it with his club, but Jack had put a sack of bran there, that was lying in the room.

At breakfast next morning, the giant said, " Pray, how did you sleep?"

" Pretty well, but for the rats," said Jack.

The giant then filled two bowls with porridge; Jack ladled his into a leather bag inside his waistcoat, and then said,

" Look here; see what I can do!"—and cutting the bag, the porridge fell on the floor.

" I can do that too!" roared the giant, and with his knife ripped his own stomach up, and died on the spot.

Soon after this, Jack was invited to King Arthur's Court, and while he was there the King's son asked him to go with him to attack a huge giant, who was the terror of one part of the country. When the Prince and his little friend arrived at the giant's castle, the former concealed himself behind a tree, while Jack boldly knocked at the castle gate.

" Who is there?" growled a voice of thunder.

" Only a weary traveller," said Jack.

" Well, then, what news do you bring ? "

" Oh, very bad ! King Arthur's son is coming here with a powerful army, to burn your castle and to put you to death ! "

" Pray come in, take my keys, and hide me in the deep stone cellar till they are gone ! "

As soon as the giant was safe under lock and key, Jack let the Prince and his followers into the castle, and they set to work to brick up the entrance to the stone cellar, so that the giant was soon starved to death.

The Prince rewarded Jack with many precious gifts, and amongst these was his own sword, which he begged his little companion to wear for his sake, and to use it in destroying wicked giants wherever he should encounter them.

After parting from the Prince, Jack passed near a forest, and fancied he heard groans coming from the trees. On drawing near, he saw a huge giant dragging by the hair a knight and lady whom he had captured. Jack had now a fair chance for making use of the sword the Prince had given him, and having quietly approached, he dealt the giant so well-aimed a blow across the legs, that he fell to the ground, when Jack quickly dispatched him, and released the captives.

Jack learned that the giant just killed by him had a

brother with a hideous great head on a small body, who was so savage that the very sight of him, with his frightful club covered with iron spikes, was enough to terrify people to death. Although this monster was almost more than his match, Jack was not daunted, and he watched at the mouth of the cave where the giant lived, until he should come out. And he did come out by-and-bye, with a horrid roar, rolling his great eyes and grinding his teeth ; Jack then, by a thrust through his right arm, disabled him, and after this he soon found an opportunity to finish him.

After this the knight and his lady invited Jack to their castle, where they gave a grand feast in his honour. But while they were all enjoying themselves, a servant, who could scarcely speak for fright, came to say that a fierce giant with two heads, named Thundel, was coming, and that he was now very close. At this even the bravest of the knights present shook with fear ; but Jack told them to take courage, and he would show them how to deal with the giant. He then ordered the drawbridge, which crossed the moat that ran round the knight's castle, to be nearly sawn through. By this time the giant had arrived, and Jack went out to meet him. After leading him a dance round the castle, so that all the lords and ladies might see him, Jack ran lightly over the drawbridge. The giant attempted to follow him, but the bridge, being sawn in the middle, gave

way beneath his immense weight, and he fell plump into the water, where Jack soon made an end of him.

There now remained only one giant to be got rid of, who held a Duke's daughter among his captives. Jack was determined to rescue this fair lady, although it was a task of very great danger; for the giant's gate was guarded by two fiery dragons, at the sight of which hideous monsters he, for the first time, felt a little afraid. But this did not last long; he soon took courage again, and coming close up to the gate, found there was a huge horn, under which these words were written—

> Whoever can this trumpet blow,
> Will cause the giant's overthrow.

Jack now took a long breath, and manfully blew the horn; the gates flew open, and in a moment the giant, his castle, and the dragons turned into a blue mist, and were no more to be seen. Nothing remained but the captives: amongst these was the Duke's beautiful daughter, who soon after was given by her father in marriage to our brave little hero, Jack—a reward he fully deserved, for being so famous a giant-killer.

PATTY AND HER PITCHER

PATTY AND HER PITCHER;

OR, KINDNESS OF HEART.

PATTY was the most charming little girl in her native village, and so all the neighbours said. Such a character as this it is very difficult to obtain; but when children do get it, you may be sure they deserve it. Patty deserved it, for she loved everybody and everything; and, in return, she was rewarded by the love of all who knew her. The pigeons flew down from their little house to coo round her; the fowls fed from her hand; the cat rolled over her feet, and purred out her fondness; and even the steady old dog Bluff amused himself with the strangest antics and gambols whenever he could gain her attention. They all knew very well how kind and good she was, although they could not say so.

She was also very industrious; for when quite a child, she used to bustle about and do little things in the handiest manner; and as for sewing, she was the pattern child at the dame's school, where her sampler was hung up in state, that the other children should see what might be done by industry and care.

When she went to the spring that was near, to dip her pitcher into its bright bubbling water, she would warble out her sweet little ballads with a voice that took the attention of all who heard, for her heart was full of joy, and she could not restrain her gladness. On one of her journeys to the spring happened the great event of her life, which I now sit down to write. It will show very clearly that we should always be ready to do a kind action to any one, for love and kindness shown to others always return tenfold to the giver, as it did to her.

Well, then, to begin the story, as I have now told you all about Patty and her goodness. Patty had filled her pitcher at the spring, and was carrying it home (and it was no trifle to carry when full), when, almost in sight of her cottage, she saw a poor old woman sitting upon the trunk of a fallen tree, as if fatigued after a long journey. Her face was as brown as a nut, and covered with wrinkles, and her eyes were dull and sunken. On her back was tied a bundle, heavy enough for a strong man to carry. She turned her eyes upon

157

Patty as she approached, and cast eager looks upon the sparkling water in the pitcher, a draught from which she longed to ask for; and trusting in the good-natured rosy face of Patty, she at last ventured to do so.

"Dear little child," said she, in a feeble voice, "let me cool my parched lips with a drink from your pitcher, for I am very old, and faint, and weary."

"To be sure, mother, and welcome," said Patty, lifting it up so that the old woman might readily quench her thirst.

Long and eagerly did the poor creature drink: so long, indeed, that Patty was really quite surprised.

"Thank you, my darling. Heaven will reward you for your kindness to the poor and aged," said the old woman.

"Oh! you 're quite welcome, mother," replied Patty, and again went on her way; but she had not proceeded far before she met a large dog, who seemed to be bound on a long journey, for he was covered with dust, his eyes were red, and his parched tongue was hanging out of his mouth, to catch the cool air. "Poor fellow!" said Patty.

The dog turned round at her kind voice, and stopped to look at her; she held out her hand, and he came near her; she put down her pitcher to caress him, and then he tried to make his way to what his instinct told him was water : she knew what the poor dog wanted, and held the pitcher so that he could drink. He lapped and lapped until she really began to think that he would never leave off. At last he looked up to her face, and licked her hand in gratitude ; then, after two or three bounds, to show her how refreshed he was, he trotted on his way.

Soon after, she met a group of little children who had been gathering flowers and daisies, and making posies with them. They had been scampering about the fields, and were tired and thirsty. So Patty told them to put their little hands together, and make cups of them ; then she filled these "handy cups," and made them drink.

"Will you please take this nosegay ? " they said, and offered her the prettiest one they had.

"Let me put it in your bosom myself," said the smallest one of the group. Patty stooped down while the grateful child fastened it with a pin to her frock. Each of them received a kiss, and then all ran off to pluck more pretty flowers.

Patty looked into her pitcher, and found that it was more than half empty, so that she must have all her journey over again, for it was of no use going home with such a drop as that. But then she saw some harebells growing by the dusty road-side, drooping for want of water, so she gave them the benefit of what was left in her pitcher, and the flowers seemed to love her for her kindness.

Back she went, without one thought about her trouble, and soon gained the margin of the spring. She was just about to stoop, and dip her pitcher into its transparent depth, when she thought she saw something glistening beneath, which caused her to withdraw her hand. She watched and watched, until she saw a sweet little face looking up to her ; and presently there stood before her one of the most beautiful of Fairies. She stood upon the water with the same ease as Patty stood on the land, and she was not really higher than the pitcher.

"So Patty," said she—you see, she knew Patty—"so you have come back again, my dear ! "

"Yes, madam," replied Patty, rather alarmed ; "yes, madam, because I——"

"I know all about it," said the Fairy, stopping her ; "and because I know, is the reason that you see me ; for I am a friend only to the good and kind ; and I come now to make you a very useful present."

"A present ! " said Patty, surprised and pleased.

"Yes! and such a one as will be a lasting reward for your good-ness of heart towards others, and your little care about yourself. You blush, because you do not remember the many kind things that you have done, and I am the more pleased to see that you think I am giving you too much praise. You forget all those acts of kindness which are the ornament of your life, and this assures me of the pureness of your motives; for it is our duty to forget the good we do to others, and to remember only what they do for us. You have always done so, my dear little Patty. To reward you I will place a spell upon your pitcher, which, for the future, shall always be full of water, or of milk, as you may wish it. It shall also be able to walk and to speak whenever you may require it, and shall always be your firm friend in trouble. Trust to it, and never give way to despair. If, by any mishap, it should be parted from you, it will easily, by its magic power, be able to find you, and be by your side as your adviser and protector. Do not be afraid to accept this at my hands, for I am one of the Fairies who oppose all that is evil. You, by your goodness, have acquired the power of seeing me and hearing me speak. Whenever mortals are good enough, this power is given to them, and we appear, and present them with some reward that only the virtuous deserve on this earth. So put your pitcher down by your side, Patty." Patty did as she was desired. "Now look into it."

Patty did so, and, to her astonishment, beheld the bright water gradually rising until the pitcher was full to the brim. When she saw it was full she was going to raise it, but found it too heavy for her strength.

"You need not trouble yourself to carry it," said the Fairy, smiling; "it will itself save you all further trouble of that kind."

With that she touched it with her wand, and the pitcher raised itself upon two very well-shaped legs, made out of the same stone as the brown pitcher itself. As soon as it was firm on its feet, it made a very polite bow to Patty as its future mistress.

"Now, Patty," said the Fairy, "follow your pitcher, and you cannot do wrong."

As she finished speaking, she broke into thousands of sparkling drops, and mixed with the bubbling stream, which seemed to bear her away.

Patty rubbed her eyes, in hopes that she should wake from what really appeared a dream. She coughed aloud, then pinched herself, then ran up and down the lane, and at last she was convinced she was awake. But more than all, there stood the brown pitcher on his natty brown legs, waiting for orders what to do.

"Quite ready to start, mistress," said a voice from the pitcher. Patty screwed up her courage, and said, "Come on, then, pitcher," and set the example by starting off with a run.

And did not the pitcher follow her in good earnest? Indeed, it ran so fast that it soon overtook her, and ran before her all the way home. But the most wonderful thing was, although it bounded along with long strides and high jumps over the roughest places in the lanes, it did not spill one single drop of water. This puzzled Patty, who, with her utmost care, could never avoid wetting her frock whenever she had tried to run with the pitcher even half full.

"What will the people think when we get into the village?"

thought Patty, as she looked at her strange companion. "I'm
sure they will be frightened; and what will my mother and father
say when they see what I have brought home?"

"Do not trouble yourself about that," said the pitcher, who
seemed to hear her thoughts: "your parents will soon get accus-
tomed to me, and be rather pleased when they discover my
handiness; for you have yet to find out all the good things I
can do."

As he was speaking, they came to a very high and difficult
stile.

"Shall I help you over?" said Patty, thinking of his short legs.

"Oh, dear, no!" said the pitcher: "see how little I require it."

So saying, he skipped over the stile in the most graceful manner. As he did so, a dog that was passing popped his tail between his legs, and after two or three very weak barks, ran away in a dreadful fright. A man, at the same time, was approaching with a slow and pompous walk—for he was the Squire of the village—who, upon perceiving the strange pitcher clear the stile in that miraculous manner, was overcome with wonder; but he soon moved pretty quickly when he saw the little legs speeding along towards him. He uttered one loud cry, and fled. His hat flew one way, his gold-headed cane another, and his cloak flew up into the air like wings. He had not proceeded far before his legs failed him, and he lay kicking in a furze-bush, roaring for help. Patty could not help laughing, but the pitcher, trotting on with the greatest unconcern, soon reached the cottage door, where he rather astonished Patty's poor parents. When he entered, he sat himself quietly down in the corner where he had been always kept, so that nobody could see his legs. The neighbours, therefore, who had been alarmed by the Squire's account of his fright, and only saw a pitcher like every one had at home, of course thought the old Squire a little bit out of his mind.

Patty was awakened next morning by hearing a noise below, as if some one were busy with the furniture. She heard the chairs pushed about, and presently the handle of a pail clinked down as plain as plain could be. So she put on part of her clothes and crept down. The noise still continuing, she peeped through the red curtains that were hung across the room to keep the wind away from their backs when they sat by the fire-side; and there she saw, not any thieves, but the pitcher; and what do you think it was doing? Why, mopping the red tiles of the floor, and very well did he handle the mop. And there was the pail full of water by his side, as if he had been a servant-of-all-work all his life; and more wonderful still, there was the fire burning! We can fancy a pitcher of water washing the floor, but cannot imagine its doing anything with a fire except putting it out. But no! there had he lighted the fire and put the kettle on, which was just singing a most delightful song about the breakfast being nearly ready.

"Good morning, my good mistress," said the pitcher, in no way put out. "You need not trouble yourself to do anything but grow and improve yourself; for from henceforth you will have very little labour to do, as I am your very humble servant."

Was not Patty pleased! for she was growing a tall girl, and felt a great desire to improve herself with her books, which she had

had very little time to do, as she had been so much occupied with her household duties.

When Patty was left alone in the evening with the pitcher in the corner, she said how much she was obliged to him, and how much she wished to learn, but wanted to know what she was to do for books, as she had read the few she possessed a hundred times.

"Oh! that's very soon remedied," said the pitcher, "for you have only to wish, and I will yield as much milk as you please. Then you can make butter and cheese, and go and sell it at the market town, and buy as many books as you like, and have plenty of money to spare for other purposes."

No sooner said than done. Patty set out all the pans she had

and could borrow from her kind neighbours; and, as fast as they came, the pitcher ran about and filled them; so that she soon had plenty of cream for her butter and cheese. She had only to ask, and a good old neighbour lent her a churn, which the pitcher soon found a pair of arms to turn; and such butter was produced as had not been seen in the village for many a day. Was not Patty pleased, and were not her parents delighted!

The same old farmer lent her a horse and panniers, and early in the morning she started for the market town, the way to which the pitcher pointed out to her. He did not go with her, as he said the people of the town were not used to see brown pitchers, so he should stop at home and look after the cheese. Patty proceeded on her

way, looking as happy and as handsome as the best farmer's daughter
of them all. So everybody in the market said, where she sold all
her butter.

So went on Patty's success until she grew into a pretty, neat,
young woman; with her old parents living in comfort in one of the
best cottages in the village; everybody saying that she deserved
her good fortune, and not one single soul envying her: you may
guess she was happy indeed.

One evening she was standing in the garden, feeding some of her
pigeons, when a handsomely-dressed stranger approached the gate,
who, after admiring her for a short time, took off his plumed hat in
the most graceful manner, and begged her to inform him the nearest

way to the next town. When she spoke, the music of her voice and her charming modesty seemed to increase the admiration of the stranger. He bowed, and, after a slight hesitation, went on his way.

But that young stranger came again and again, although he knew his way very well to and from the neighbouring city. At last she found that it was the way to her heart he was seeking; for he told her parents that he was rich, and wished to have a wife whom everybody spoke well of, since his own wealth left him at liberty to choose for himself, without a desire for any more. The parents smiled as they looked upon the handsome suitor, whom they did not think one bit too good for their dear Patty; and so in the course of a short time they were married.

Great joy was in the village on the day of the wedding. If the Queen had visited the village, there could not have been more gladness of heart. All left off work and made holiday.

Groups of people here and there talked of the kind actions Patty had done. The poor women spoke of the clothes she had made for them, and said, "there never was such a good creature as Patty." Some had received nice little dishes of cookery when they were ill. Many of the girls had been taught to sew and make garments; and the little children had been taught to read. The church was filled with people who loved her, and wished to take one last fond look at her sweet face. Garlands of flowers were hung across the road, with mottoes such as "Patty the Good," "God bless our friend Patty," "Kind actions never die." And when the married pair started from the church, scores of old shoes were flung after them for good luck, with such shouts and huzzas that the village never heard before.

But the stranger who had married Patty took her home to a noble palace, where his forefathers had reigned for many centuries as princes; and the humble little Patty found that her dear husband had made her a Princess, and surrounded her with all the luxuries and splendours of her high station.

Did Patty forget her humble home and her old friend the pitcher? No! she did not: the pitcher was with her, but her parents wished to remain in their peaceful home, which their dear child had made so happy by her virtuous industry.

In the splendid state in which Patty now lived the pitcher was as much her servant and benefactor as when he first assisted her in the humble cottage. When the poor came to the palace gates, he stood there and poured into their pitchers nourishing soup to sup-

port them and their families; and they did not forget to bless the good Princess for her kindly thoughts of those who needed her protection and charity so much; and so the pitcher, although now not called upon to work, still continued, in the name of his mistress, to do good to all around.

But even the very best of us cannot escape from envious hearts and evil tongues; and so it fell out to Princess Patty: for we love to call her Patty, although she became a Princess. Many of the wicked courtiers, who envied her being loved by the people, whispered slanders into the ears of the Prince her husband, who at last was weak enough to listen to them; for they made him afraid by telling him that she was trying to bribe the people, by

her charities, to rebel against the rightful Prince, and to place
herself on the throne alone; and also that evil spirits helped her;
and that the friendly pitcher was one of them.

Alas for human weakness! The Prince, at last, was convinced,
by their arguments, of her guilt; and, although his heart ached,
commanded her to be put into a dungeon in the very depths of the
palace, and left her there to mourn. She did not mourn long, for
as night came on, the pitcher opened her prison doors and aided
her in her flight.

"Come," said he, "return to your peaceful home, and show your
husband that it is his heart, and not his kingdom, that you covet.

He will be sorry for what he has done when he finds that he has lost you."

She followed the pitcher; but they had not proceeded far in their flight when Patty saw that they were pursued by a party of soldiers: she screamed with alarm.

"Be not alarmed, dearest mistress," said the pitcher; "I will stop these pursuers." So saying, he bent over the side of the rock and poured out a cataract of water into the valley through which they were coming. The waters rolled in high waves and swept them from the path, until it became like a large, deep lake. The soldiers swam to the nearest land, glad to save their lives.

That night she slept beneath the humble roof of her parents;

their own dear Patty. Early in the morning she was in her own beloved garden with the beautiful flowers, and she tried to be happy and forget the past, by being always at work and by making others happy ; but her thoughts would wander to the home of her husband, and she grieved over his unkindness to her, in return for her love to him ; and sometimes, in the midst of her tears, she would hope that some fortunate accident might remove the evil thought from his mind, that had caused her so much grief. The pitcher was always by her side, and gave her comfort in her silent sorrow.

The news of Patty's return to her home soon spread through the village, and all came to see once more one whom they had learned to love so much. She told them nothing of her husband's cruel conduct, for she loved him too much to let them think he was unkind.

"Our friend Patty," they said, "has come to visit her parents ; we must make her a present."

Many a talk they had about what the present should be. At last they settled it, and all the girls helped to make a beautiful piece of worsted work, wrought with many bright colours, and spread on a handsome frame. The motto worked in it was " KIND ACTIONS TO OTHERS BRING HAPPINESS TO OURSELVES."

Little did they think how much grief was then in Patty's heart. But still the motto was true, as we shall see before we finish the story.

Days and weeks rolled on, but no news reached her from her husband. Had he quite left her ? or did he believe that she had been swept away by the torrent which had so nearly drowned his soldiers ? She hoped that it was so, for then he might be mourning her as dead ; for surely he must have found, long ere this, that the wicked courtiers had spoken falsely.

One fine morning she had risen earlier than usual, for her mind was restless, and she could not sleep. She walked into the pure air, scented with the perfume of flowers, and her fevered brow was refreshed with the cool breeze. Looking round, she beheld her friend the pitcher trimming the flowers like an old gardener who knew his business.

"Good morning, fair mistress mine," said he. "You are up betimes, for the sun has hardly climbed the distant mountains to peep into our valley ; but I am glad to see you so early afoot, as you perceive that I am taking extra care with the garden, for I expect visitors to-day."

"Visitors ?" exclaimed Patty, with an inquiring look.

"Yes, visitors," said the pitcher, from whose mouth issued a low chuckling laugh. "I can hear distinctly a footstep in the distance; it comes this way. Listen! it is now near enough for mortal ears to hear."

And so it was: nearer and nearer it came. Presently the figure of a palmer appeared at the wicket gate. He entered; but when he beheld before him the figure of his long-lost Patty, he suddenly stopped, and stood quite still, like a statue of surprise. It was indeed her husband the Prince!

"That is the visitor I expected," said the pitcher: "he has believed you dead, and has wandered to many places to assuage his grief. At last he has dared to venture to this humble cottage, that

he might again see the spot where he first had the good fortune to meet you. He hoped to console his unhappy mind, and to atone for his crime, by coming where everything would remind him of you and of your virtues, and of the fault he has committed in believing that you were trying to get his riches and his kingdom, when he himself was all your world, all your riches, all your enjoyment. Your being alive is the reward for his sincere repentance. He finds you in your first humble sphere, grieving for nothing but the loss of him, hoping for nothing but the return of his love."

The Prince rushed forward with a cry of delight, and knelt at Patty's feet. The pitcher, like a discreet friend, placed her hand in his, and then went on with his gardening, leaving the long-

separated couple to themselves, who quickly effected a reconcilia-
tion with each other.

Patty's parents rejoiced in her newly-found happiness, yet felt
a pang of regret when, some days after the happy meeting, the
Prince proposed that they should return to his kingdom, and that
he would send forward a message that his wife should make her
entry in triumph.

The pitcher walked out of the cottage and joined the group.

"Prince," said he, "spare yourself the trouble. I am here to give my
last service to my mistress. I have rewarded her for the greatest
of virtues, *self-denial* and *love for her fellow-creatures*, and the Fairy
who animated me now recalls me to her water palace : behold !"

As he ceased speaking, jets of sparkling water rose high into the air from his mouth, until a broad lake spread over the valley, upon which was borne a gilded barge, rowed by stout boatmen in the Prince's livery. It glided to their feet, and they all stepped in. The servants pulled with a good will into the midst of the stream. Still the fountain played from the pitcher's mouth until the stream was swollen into a mighty river, down which they floated until they came in sight of their own castle, standing high up on the rocks on the border of the current. Flags floated from the turrets, and booming cannon sent forth their noisy welcome. Crowds of rejoicing vassals stood to receive their much-loved Princess, whose happy tears spoke for her to the hearts that knew so well how good she was. The Prince and Princess lived happily many years over a thriving and contented people, whose love and loyalty were the strongest bulwarks of their throne. The benevolence of the Princess, and her charming courtesy and gentleness, gained her the title of " The Gentle Princess," and she was pointed out as a model for the imitation of all the young princesses of the neighbouring countries.

The happy pair were blessed with a numerous and beautiful family of sons and daughters, to whom their mother would often relate the story of her early life; for she was not ashamed to confess her former lowly station and humble parentage; and much wonder and delight was always expressed by the younger children at her account of the magic pitcher, and many were the wishes that it would again make its appearance; but these wishes were not to be gratified. The magic pitcher was seen no more; but its history teaches all who read it that

KINDNESS TO OTHERS BRINGS HAPPINESS TO OURSELVES.

PETER AND HIS GOOSE;

OR, THE FOLLY OF DISCONTENT.

THERE was once a little boy named Peter, whose father and mother died, and left him an orphan. Having no relations, he was quite his own master; and although he grieved for the death of his kind parents, he felt pleased that now there was no one to set him tasks or to prevent his wandering about the pleasant fields enjoying his idle hours. All this he could afford to do, for his parents had been very careful of their money, and had owned a pretty little farm, well stocked with all kinds of chickens, and ducks, and geese, and sheep, and corn and hay; and they had left all these to Peter. But the little fellow had forgotten that there must be industry and attention in the master, or he could not expect to thrive. He, however, lived at his ease, and never troubled himself to look forward to the morrow. He slept in the sunshine, and, when that was gone, he went indoors and slept in his bed: so, you see, we can't say much in favour of little Peter. But you shall hear the end of all this, and how he was taught to do better.

He was one day lying in the sunshine, thinking of nothing but his dinner, when a solemn old goose walked up to him, and said, in a plain, clear, and distinct voice,

"Master Peter, how d' ye do?"

Peter turned round and opened his eyes very wide, for he was rather surprised. But he mustered up courage, and said,

"Thank you, Mrs. Goose, I'm pretty well;" and wondered what was to come next, for a goose talking was enough to cause even Peter to stare.

"That's right! keep wide awake this time," said the goose, "for I have much to say that rather concerns you. You must know that I am a fairy bird, and I lay very wonderful eggs, for any person having one can become what he wishes when he breaks it: he may be changed into a bird, or a fish, or a king, or anything else. But I can lay only fifteen eggs for one person, and that number I have already in the nest; so, you lucky fellow, go and begin wishing directly."

No sooner had the goose ceased speaking than Peter slowly raised himself, for he was so lazy that not even this good luck could make him move quickly, and seeking the nest, found that the eggs were there, and that the goose had really spoken the truth.

"Now, what do you say?" said the goose, who had waddled after him.

"Ah! but I must try first," exclaimed Peter, "for I can hardly believe you."

"Take an egg, and smash it on the ground," continued the old goose, "first wishing to be something."

"Ah! but what?" said Peter.

"Well!" said the goose, "if you take my advice, you would wish to be a bird, for it is a very nice thing to be a bird, I can tell you."

"To be sure," said Peter, "so here goes: I wish to be a bird." As he said so, he broke the egg upon the stones, when his wooden shoes flew off, and his hat spun in the air, and down he fell on his back, in the shape of a gigantic stork; but very uncomfortable he felt: his great beak kept snapping, and his long legs kept slipping, until he screamed with fright.

"Oh dear! oh dear! I won't stand this! I won't be a bird! I wish to be Peter again!" shouted he. And he was Peter again in a minute; and didn't he pop on his hat and shoes in a hurry?

"You see," said the goose, with a very wise shake of the head, "you left it to chance what bird you would turn to; you ought to have thought a little first, and fixed upon one you would have liked: some birds live pleasanter lives than others."

"Ah! I shan't be any bird," said Peter, rather in a sulky humour, for he felt sore with his falls. "I will be a something grand: a soldier, now, like those who passed through the village last week."

With that, down went another egg; but, strange to say, the cracking was dreadful, and, moreover, it grew louder and louder, until it became like the roaring of cannon. And, indeed, so it was; for there was Peter in the midst of a great battle, with the cannon-balls and bomb-shells flying about him, and he running about like one mad, to escape from them as they exploded. Peter was dressed as a soldier; but he had none of the soldier's bravery in his heart, and he trembled as he found himself in the trenches before a terrible fortress that blazed out death and destruction upon those attacking it. A shell burst very near to him and blew him some yards off, covered with dust and smoke; it was a great wonder that he was not killed outright.

"Oh! I wish I was well out of this," said he, as his helmet was knocked off with a bullet. Down he fell upon his back, and up he rose again simple Peter, in his own farm-yard, and the old goose staring at him. He wiped the dust and sweat from his brow and smacked his lips, for his mouth was now quite dry with fright and the gunpowder. At that moment his eyes fell upon some very tempting fruit in a neighbour's garden.

"Oh! don't I wish I was up that tree, and my hat full of apples." He caught up an egg and broke it, and he was up in the tree surrounded with apples. "Now," said he, "I'll enjoy myself; I'm fond of apples, and I'll have a feast."

He began to eat as fast as he could, filling his hat at the same time with as many as it would hold, that he might carry them home. But silly Peter had no time to enjoy his plunder; for right under him stood the angry master of the orchard, with a heavy whip in his hand, which he applied with a right good will to the back of the eater of his apples. Peter lost very little time in wishing himself back at home, where he found himself directly, the goose asking him "why he shrugged his shoulders so?"

"What a heavy whip the farmer has!" said he; "he nearly killed me."

That evening Peter and the goose sat together, employing them-

selves for some considerable time in talking about what was best to
be done.

"A lucky thought!" said Peter suddenly. "I will have lots of
money; then shan't we be happy?" As he spoke, he saw the lid
of his corn-bin open, and upon looking in he saw it was filled with
shining gold. They both looked at it till the night came on, when
Peter got the largest padlock he could find and put it on the door,
for he began to fear thieves, poor fellow!—he had never feared them
before. After this he could not sleep, but looked out of the window
at the moonlight, thinking every sound he heard was the step of some
one coming to rob him, and the goose walked up and down outside

as sentinel. In the morning he amused himself again with the gold, counting it out in little heaps, spreading it over the table, and making figures with the sovereigns; but hearing some footsteps outside, he hastily flung it all into the bin, and slammed down the lid, which caught Peter's hand and gave it a most fearful squeeze.

Peter, although he was not very wise, began to find that this was a very foolish way of enjoying himself; so, as the sentinel goose came near the window, he said,

"I say, Mrs. Goose, this is rather stupid work, I think: don't you know any means whereby we can be rich, and have some one else

to guard our treasure, and only look at it ourselves when we want
to take some of it?"

"Well!" replied the goose, "what do you say to being a King?
the only trouble they have is how to spend money."

"Ah! I never thought of that," said Peter; "I'll be a King, see
if I don't."

With that he opened the cottage door and smashed an egg, and
in an instant stood in a grand hall, with a very stiff ruff round his
neck, a very heavy crown on his head, and a very long tail to his
robe. Here everybody bowed to him, but he simply asked them
what time dinner would be ready. They replied that it would be

served about eight o'clock, which, when Peter was Peter, was his supper-time.

"How shall I spend the time till then?" he thought. "I'll play at nine-pins!"

So he looked round about among the fine people in the palace, and shook hands with some very tall men in livery, dressed in scarlet and gold lace, thinking them to be the grandees of the palace, and asked them to come and play with him; and seeing some one in plain black, by no means new, he fancied he was the right man for errands, so he told him to be quick and fetch the pins and balls. But the gentleman in black, who was the Prime Minister, the highest man in the country next to the King, went and talked to his friends, and they all said, "This is not a proper king to rule over us; we must cut off his head." Then they brought some soldiers, and went to Peter and told him he should not be King more than two days longer, and that it was not proper for the King to play at nine-pins with the footmen in the palace. When they had gone out, the goose made a very low bow to his kingship, and asked him how he felt.

"Well!" said Peter, "if being King means doing what everybody else wishes, and not to do what I want myself, and not being allowed to have a game of nine-pins, and dining late, I shall abdicate; for, to tell you the truth, I want to lie on the grass and dine directly off the knuckle of ham that I know is in the cupboard at home; so, goose, get out of the way, and let me wish myself back again."

"Stop!" says the goose, "I brought one of the eggs with me this morning; so, perhaps, you would like to try something else before you go home to the ham-bone."

"Well! upon my word, I hardly know," said Peter, with a very doubtful look. "I am quite puzzled; but where is the egg?"

"Under your Majesty's chair," replied the goose.

Peter stooped with a great deal of trouble, in his stiff dress, and picked up the egg.

"I think," said he, as he rose, "an admiral of a fleet seems about the best sort of fellow. I know he is always roving about to foreign parts, on the beautiful sea, and really does pretty much as he likes, and wears a very nice uniform."

Down went the egg; and, behold! Peter was an admiral, with a patch over his eye, a hook at the end of one arm, and a furious pain in his left toe, and was propped up with a very handsome crutch.

"Oh dear! oh dear!" exclaimed Peter, "I didn't mean an old admiral: here's a pretty deception!"

"I think," said the goose, "that they do not make young admirals to go to sea; they sometimes do when they are to stay at home."

A storm came on just then, and Peter had to stop on deck for twelve hours without his dinner, eating only some very hard biscuit. A wave broke over the deck and dashed him against the mast, which knocked out some more of his teeth, and nearly washed him overboard.

"This won't do for me," said Peter; "I wonder how any one can

be fond of being at sea. I shall wish myself back again." He did
so, and found himself standing in his own room at home, with the
old goose on the table before him.

Poor Peter was in a passion, and drew out his knife to cut off the
head of the poor goose who had brought him to such trouble. But
she was not going to be killed so easily. She screamed as loudly
as he talked, and said he was ungrateful for the favours she had
bestowed, which would have helped others with more brains to have
become rich and famous; so that at last she had the best of it, and
talked him into a calmer humour.

"You must make yourself wiser by travel," said she. "I have

often seen you reading books of travel with much pleasure.   Pray,
why do you not make yourself the hero of one such book ? "

"That's not a bad idea," said Peter, who was now in a good
temper. "Suppose I was to turn a kind of Robinson Crusoe, and
have an island all to myself?   I'll do it ! I'll do it ! " said he, quite
jolly at the notion.   He took up an egg, and crushed it with his
foot.

He was sitting on an island, with the wind and the sea raging
around him, and the storm-birds wheeling and screaming above his
head.   There sat Peter, the cast-away sailor, on his island.   Such
an island ! about six feet square ; just room enough to say that

he was high and dry, with the waves making snatches at him, as if eager to roll him over and over into the deep below. Some hungry sharks, too, helped to spoil his quiet, rushing all round the rock, staring at Peter as if ready to make a meal of him.

"Oh! miserable wretch that I am," exclaimed Peter, shivering with cold and fright, "how shall I get home? I can only do it as a fish; but I can't say that I should like to be under the water. But I need not, for I can be a flying-fish, and that I will be."

He took out an egg and broke it, when he felt his ears growing into long transparent fins, and his legs kicking out in the strangest manner, when a power he could not oppose made him glide into the water, where he floated most pleasantly for a few moments; but only for a few moments, for soon a fish twenty times his own size, with a mouth that looked like a dark cavern, and eyes that glittered like burning lamps through the bright water, prepared to swallow him for his lunch. Out flew poor Peter from this terrible enemy, and used his new wings with great effect, for they bore him many yards above the rolling sea.

"I am safe now," said Peter, who dipped upon the very tops of the waves every few minutes to rest his wings. Again he rose, thinking he had made a wise change this time, when a scream of startling shrillness sounded from above, which, upon turning his eye, he saw proceeded from a fierce-looking sea-bird, which was making at him with open beak to snap him up. This was not the worst; for twenty more like him followed in a long line, all intent upon the same amiable purpose of swallowing the poor flying-fish. Down popped Peter; up popped the big fish with the large mouth; up popped Peter; scream went the birds who were waiting for their food.

"Murder!" exclaimed Peter; "I only wish I was out of this." And out of it he was at his wish, running at full speed along the highway towards his home, which he soon reached in a most breathless state. Flinging open the gate, he beheld the old goose, who, with a dreadful cackle, fell over with fright at his appearance, for Peter had not, strange to say, quite finished his change back again to himself, so that the poor goose had just cause to be frightened, for he still had the head of the flying-fish, which did not change to his own till after he had been at home an hour or more. This last adventure had pretty nearly cured Peter of break-ing any more of the charmed goose's eggs, although his mind would sometimes wander towards them, with strange wishes about things that he really knew nothing of; but, like all idle people, he would

dream about all sorts of odd projects.   Not any of them, however, had any labour or trouble on his part mixed up with them.

He wandered about his farm with the old waddling goose, who cackled on, all day, a wonderful deal of nonsense, as all old geese will ; but he did not make up his mind to break another egg until, quite wearied with the fatigue of nothing to do, he resolved to have just one more little try.   But what was it to be ?   No bird with long stilted legs, no soldier to be shot, no money to keep him in a state of alarm, no kings with late dinners and uncomfortable clothes, no admiral with only half himself left, no island of small size, no fish with enemies in the air and the water ; none of these, but something with plenty to eat and drink, and nothing to do. As he thought all this, his ears were saluted with a loud grunt, which issued from a stye at his back. He looked over the gate, and beheld a picture of luxury and idleness—a fine fat pig, lying in the clean straw, with its eyes half shut, and its ears just moving enough to frighten away the flies.

"Ah! my fine fellow," said Peter, "you are happy indeed! you have nothing to do, and you have plenty of food, without the trouble of working for it. Oh! you are the very chap I should like to be!" Without more ado, he seized an egg and smashed it against the wall. He at once rolled down into the clean straw, a perfect pig, a model of fatness, sleek as the egg he had broken to procure the happy change.

He grunted with pleasure as he stretched his limbs to the grateful warmth of the sun, and he munched, with relish, a few fine apples that had fallen from a tree above his dwelling, and he gave himself up to the most delicious dreams, as pigs and lazy people will do.

The door of his stye was unbolted, and a man of queer appearance entered Peter's straw-chamber, and commenced poking his large horny fingers into his ribs.

"What is this fellow about now?" thought Peter. He would have said, "Be quiet, do!" only, as a pig, he could not, although it tickled him very much; for Peter, as Peter, could not bear anybody to tickle him—and Peter, as a pig, was quite as tender about his ribs.

Still the man kept on his poking and pinching, humming a tune in the coolest manner, as if the pig had no feeling.

At last he began tucking up his sleeves, as if about to do something. Now, as this had something to do with Peter the pig, he opened both his eyes, so that he should see what was going on. The man took no notice of his opening his eyes; but, to the horror of poor Peter, he pulled out a knife of the most murderous look, and held it in his mouth; then, seizing poor Peter by the ears, pulled him round, and, after feeling him about the throat, the butcher prepared to finish him on the spot.

Peter was not longer than what is called "the twinkling of an eye" wishing himself out of his four legs into his two; and as soon as he found himself changing into Peter, he tried his voice.

"I'm not a pig!" screamed Peter; "what are you going to do with that knife?"

The knife dropped from the butcher's hand; his trembling knees

could hold the pig no longer; he scrambled out upon his hands
and knees until he got clear of the stye; he then rose upon his legs,
and made off as fast as he could.   Peter seized the knife, and ran
after him, to give him, in turn, a taste of its sharpness.

   The butcher screamed as he saw a man pursuing him with a real
pig's head, and a large knife in his hand.   So frightened was he that
he fell into the brook, and was nearly drowned; at which, Peter,
who just then found his own head on his shoulders, which was more
convenient to laugh with, burst into a loud fit of laughter.

   Peter walked home, and had supper with the old goose.

   " Goose," said he, " I will be something pretty next time, for I

am tired of beasts, birds, and fishes. Now, as a friend, what would you really advise me to do, that would not turn out in any way unpleasant?"

"Upon my word," said the goose, "I really don't know; for whatever it is, you see, you will change more slowly as you come to the end of the eggs; and it may not be agreeable, in some cases, to grow by slow degrees into the shape of any strange creature."

"You are right," replied Peter, "for I have found the changes slower every time. But I was thinking that a butterfly is a pretty light character to sustain, without much fatigue; and then the lodging is pleasant, being usually the bosom of some fragrant flower.

Now, what do you think of a handsome butterfly? I should then be a credit to my own garden."

"Well, upon my word!" again said the goose, who had become rather fearful of giving advice; "I should say that I would do as I felt if I were you;" thus leaving the matter to be settled by Peter himself.

Peter had his own way, and took out the last egg but one, which he broke, but not so briskly as before, wishing himself, at the same time, a handsome butterfly. He was sitting on a three-legged stool, with the old goose opposite to him.

"Now your horns are growing," said the old goose, "and your wings are sprouting out finely; they are really splendid. How do you feel?"

"Very unpleasant indeed," said Peter. "Oh, my gracious, how it hurts! oh, my back! oh, my forehead! oh, my legs! how little they are—oh!"

Here he left off, for his head was a butterfly's; and soon his whole body changed, and he was a splendid butterfly.

"This is charming," said butterfly Peter, as he flew about in the sunshine, and every moment popped into some delicious flower. "I'm sure I shall keep as I am."

"But there is one thing to remember," said the goose: "your life will be a short and a merry one; for butterflies, I have heard say, are what mortals call the 'beings of a day,' which, I suppose, means that they only live twelve hours. Now, if that be the case, my poor master, you will have very little time to enjoy yourself, and I shall have to mourn your death at sunset."

The butterfly Peter stopped. "Good gracious!" said he, "I remember that what you hint at is true, and I have been fool enough to trouble myself with a change that will last me for so short a time; and how do I know that I may not die before I get out of this pleasant form?"

"Don't you think you had better wish yourself back, Peter?" said the goose.

"Directly, of course," said Peter; "do you take me for a fool?"

"Not quite," replied the goose, with a rather sly look for a goose, "but I should advise you not to be long about it."

With that Peter began wishing very hard, but it was some hours before he got rid of his butterfly suit which he had so rashly assumed; and the last gleam of the sun saw him walking home as himself, with the goose by his side.

When Peter arose the next morning, he remembered that he had

only one egg left; so, of course, he felt very unwilling to throw away the last egg, which now appeared so precious to him. He sat down on a bank and considered what he should do.

"What are you thinking of?" said the goose, who had followed him without being seen.

"Why, I was thinking what I should wish with the last egg," replied he.

"Oh, don't trouble yourself," exclaimed the goose, "you have no choice; you will break it without knowing what you will turn into. Whatever that will be, you will have no control over it. But you may wish, or not wish, as you think proper; so pray don't ask me my advice, in case it might lead to anger between us."

"Whatever it turns out to be, I don't care," said Peter, in an ill temper. "Perhaps, as I have no choice, it may be for the better. I should like to see what I shall turn to, and I should be miserable with this horrid last egg unbroken. I have it here in my pocket, so that it is handy, and I will break it while I feel in the humour."

As he spoke, he dashed it from him, and he directly felt thousands of feathers pricking over his skin. He slipped off the bank upon a pair of very short legs, and his eyes showed him a long yellow nose. Quite bewildered, he cried out to the old goose, "What am I?"

"A goose! a goose! a goose!" screamed the old bird, and then went off into shouts of laughter. Peter's blood boiled with passion.

"What do you mean by scoffing at me in this manner?" shouted Peter, with great wrath.

"Why, really," replied the goose, as soon as she recovered her breath, "you are such a dreadfully awkward goose, you waddle so frightfully! but pray excuse my laughing, for could you see yourself, you would laugh too."

Peter waddled off, quite humbled, into the barn, and he didn't come out till he was quite himself again. He could not sleep at all that night, but thought of his own folly, and vowed he would mend his ways. He had found that every sort of life he had tried had its own troubles, and that it was vain to hope for any without them. "I'll be content with my present state," thought he; "I'll attend to my work, and do my duty, and if I am not so happy as I should wish, I know that others are worse off than myself, and that I shall not improve by trying to change."

The morning saw him with his scythe across his shoulder, prepared to labour in the fields that his kind parents had left him.

"Good morning, Peter," said the old goose; "where are you off so early? And you are going to work too, I declare! Oh dear! oh dear! wonders will never cease."

"Foolish bird," said Peter, "go to the common and mix with your fellows. I have come to my reason, and see my folly in neglecting the good given to me by Providence, and in wasting my time in seeking nothing but trouble and vexation; always craving after what I was not, instead of attending to what I was; and, above all, taking the advice of a goose for my guidance. I have made up my mind, I will dream no more. I will follow the example of my good parents, and I feel assured that I shall henceforth have nothing to wish for."

So saying, Peter walked out into the fields, and worked as an industrious young farmer should, and as he grew up to man's estate,
he kept to his business and became rich. Some foolish persons once
advised him to do something with his money that would make him
rich and happy without working for it, and with as much ease as
breaking an egg.

"Oh, no! thank you," said Peter, "I have broken eggs enough;
I shall break no more except those which I eat for breakfast."

PUSS IN BOOTS.

————o————

THERE was once a poor miller, who had three sons; and, when he was about to die, he left the mill to the eldest, his donkey to the second, and to the youngest boy only his cat. This last, poor fellow! thought himself very badly off in comparison with his brothers, who, by joining their property together, he would say, could get on very well; but as he had nothing but Pussy, he feared he should really starve.

Now, it happened that the cat, one day, overheard him making this complaint; so he came up, and thus spoke to his young master:

"Pray do not grieve at your lot—that is not right, you know; but trust in me, and I will do all I can to help you. Give me a bag, and get a pair of boots made for me, that I may make my way well through the mire and the brambles, and you will soon see what I can do."

The poor youth was too sad to heed Pussy's speech much; but still he got the bag and the little boots made for

him, not thinking anything would come of it, for all the cat's fine speech.

No sooner had Puss put on the boots and placed the bag on his neck, than he bade his master good morning, and boldly started off to the woods. The sly-boots had put some parsley in his bag, that he might tempt some rabbits in a warren he knew of, close by, to come and take a taste of it. Poor little things! they were too simple to suppose he meant mischief; so he very soon coaxed a nice plump young rabbit to have a nibble, and the moment he put his little nose in the bag, Puss drew the string tight, and killed him, and one or two more in the same way.

Puss was very proud of the good sport he had had, and went straight off to the Court, when he asked to speak to the King. When he came before the monarch, who was seated on a throne, with the Princess his daughter by his side, he made a graceful bow, and said,

" Please your Majesty, I have brought this game from the warren belonging to my master, the Marquis of Carabas, who desired me to lay it, with his loyal respects and offers of service, at your Majesty's feet."

Sly Puss! he had himself given his poor master that

202

grand title. The King, much pleased at this mark of homage, graciously accepted the gift, and sent his thanks to the Marquis.

One fine morning, not long after this, Puss heard that the King was going to take a ride by the river's side, with his lovely daughter; so he said to his master,

"If you only follow my advice, your fortune is made. Take off your clothes, and get into the river to bathe, just where I shall point out, and leave the rest to me."

The young man did as he was bid, without being in the least able to guess what the cat meant. While he was bathing very coolly, the King and the royal party passed by, and Puss in Boots, running after them, called out, as loud as he could bawl, "Help! help! my Lord the Marquis of Carabas is in danger of being drowned!"

The King, seeing it was the same cat that had brought him the game, sent some of his servants to assist the poor Marquis.

Puss then told his Majesty, that while his Lordship was bathing, some thieves had stolen his clothes—which was not true, for Master Puss had hidden them behind a tree, a little way off.

The King accordingly sent to the palace for a rich Court suit for him to put on, which became him very much, and he looked so handsome that the King's daughter fell in love with him, and the King made him get into the coach.

The cat, glad to find that his plan had succeeded so well, ran on before them, and seeing some reapers who were reaping in a corn-field, he said to them,

"You, good people, who are reaping, if you do not say that all this corn belongs to my Lord the Marquis of Carabas, you shall be all cut into pieces as small as minced-meat!"

The King, who passed by a minute afterwards, wished to know to whom all those corn-fields belonged. "To my Lord the Marquis of Carabas," repeated the reapers.

The cat, who ran before the coach, uttered the same threat to all he met with, and the King was astonished at the great wealth of my Lord the Marquis of Carabas.

Soon after they arrived at a grand castle, in which an ogre lived.

But Pussy slipped in before them, and was soon quite chatty with the ogre, saying, "Can't you change yourself into any animal you please?"

"Of course I can," said he; and in a moment he became a roaring lion.

The cat rushed away in alarm; but when he came back again, no lion was to be seen—only the ogre.

Puss then said, "Please do change into a mouse now."

But no sooner had he done so, than the cat sprang upon him, and ate him up.

Puss in Boots, hearing the royal party approach, went out to meet them, and bowing to the King, said,

"Your Majesty is right welcome to the castle of the Marquis of Carabas!"

The King was delighted to find his Lordship had so noble a castle, and gladly accepted the invitation to view it.

The young Marquis gave his hand to the Princess as she alighted, and both followed the King as he entered the great hall, when they all, soon after, partook of a rich feast, which the ogre had prepared for some of his own friends, little thinking how he should be himself eaten up by a cat.

The King was quite charmed with all he saw, and he liked the young Marquis more and more, not only because he was so rich, and had so grand a castle and so fine an estate; but because he was both good and wise; and he

208

soon noticed also how much the Princess was in love with the handsome youth. So he said to him,

" My dear Marquis, it will be your own fault if you do not become my son-in-law : my daughter loves you, and you have my full consent."

The Marquis was overjoyed at this great mark of royal favour, and was united to his fair bride the very next day.

You may be sure that his old friend Puss in Boots was not forgotten. That clever cat became a great favourite at Court, was richly dressed, and had such choice dainties for his food that he never again touched rats and mice. His greatest pleasure was to lounge by the balcony, on a couch, and look out on the park, when his young master and the Princess were walking in its shady groves; and Puss in Boots lived thus happily to a good old age.

LITTLE RED RIDING-HOOD AND THE WICKED WOLF.

———o———

ONCE upon a time a nice little girl lived in a country village, and she was the sweetest creature that ever was seen; her mother loved her with great fondness, and her grandmother doted on her still more. A pretty red-coloured hood had been made for the little girl, which so much became her that every one called her Little Red Riding-Hood.

One day her mother, having made some cheese-cakes, said to her,

"Go, my child, and see how your grandmother

212

does, for I hear she is ill; carry her some of these cakes, and a little pot of butter."

Little Red Riding-Hood immediately set out, with a basket filled with the cakes and the pot of butter, for her grandmother's house, which was in a village a little distant from her mother's.

As she was crossing a wood, which lay in her road, she met a wolf, who had a great mind to eat her up, but dared not indulge his wicked wish, because of some woodcutters who were at work near them in the forest.

He ventured, however, to ask her whither she was going.

The little girl, not knowing how dangerous it was to talk to a wolf, replied,

"I am going to see my grandmamma, and carry her these cakes and a pot of butter."

214

" Does she live far off ? " said the wolf.

"Oh, yes,' answered Little Red Riding-Hood, " beyond the mill you see yonder, at the first house in the village."

"Well," said the wolf, " I will go and see her too ; I will take this way, and you take that, and let us see which will be there first."

The wolf set out, running as fast as he could, and taking the nearest way ; while the little girl took the longest, and amused herself as she went with gathering nuts, running after butterflies, and making nosegays of such flowers as she found within her reach.

The wolf soon arrived at the dwelling of the grandmother, and knocked at the door.

" Who is there ? " said the old woman.

" It is your grandchild, Little Red Riding-Hood," replied the wolf, in the voice of the little girl ; " I

have brought you some cheese-cakes, and a little pot of butter, that mamma has sent you."

The good old woman, who was ill in bed, then called out,

" Pull the bobbin, and the latch will go up."

The wolf pulled the bobbin, and the door opened. He sprung upon the poor old grandmother, and ate her up in a few minutes, for it was three days since he had tasted any food.

The wolf then shut the door, and laid himself down in the bed, and waited for Little Red Riding-Hood, who very soon after reached the door.

Tap, tap!

" Who is there?"

She was at first a little frightened at the hoarse voice of the wolf, but believing her grandmother had got a cold, she answered,

" It is your grandchild, Little Red Riding-Hood. Mamma has sent you some cheese-cakes, and a little pot of butter."

The wolf called out, softening his voice,

" Pull the bobbin, and the latch will go up."

Little Red Riding-Hood pulled the bobbin, and the door opened.

When she came into the room, the wolf, hiding himself under the bed-clothes, said to her, trying all he could to speak in a feeble voice,

" Put the basket, my child, on the stool, and come close to me."

Little Red Riding-Hood accordingly stepped toward the bed; where, wondering to see how her grandmother looked in her nightclothes, she said to her,

" Grandmamma, what great arms you have got ! "

"The better to hug thee, my child."

"Grandmamma, what great ears you have got!"

"The better to hear thee, my child."

"Grandmamma, what great eyes you have got!"

"The better to see thee, my child."

"Grandmamma, what great teeth you have got!"

"They are to eat thee up!" and, saying these words, the wicked wolf was about to fall upon Little Red Riding-Hood, when a young forester, hearing her screams, rushed in and killed him with one blow of his axe.

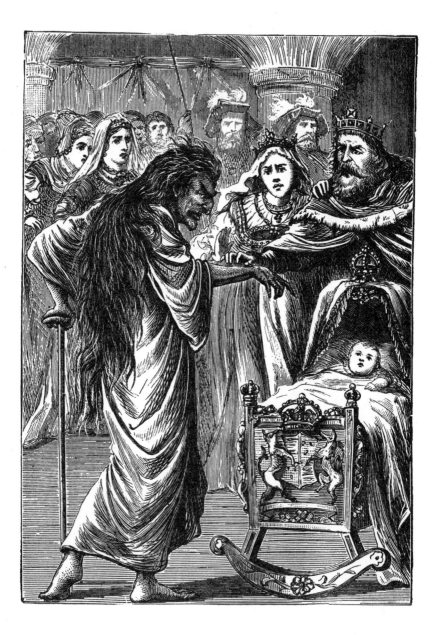

222

THE SLEEPING BEAUTY IN THE WOOD.

---o---

ONCE upon a time there was a King and Queen who were much vexed at not having any children. At length, however, a little girl was born. There was a splendid christening. For godmothers they gave the young Princess all the Fairies they could find, so that, by each making her a gift, she might become possessed of every virtue and grace. After the christening all the company returned to the King's palace, where a great banquet was set out for the Fairies. But as they were all taking their places at the table, there was seen to enter an old Fairy, who had not been invited, because for upwards of fifty years she had never quitted the tower she lived in, and it was supposed she was either dead or enchanted.

The King ordered a cover to be laid for her; but there was no possibility of giving her a massive gold case such as the others had. The old lady thought she was treated with contempt, and muttered some threats between her teeth. One of the young Fairies overheard her, and, thinking she might cast some misfortune on the little Princess, went, as soon as they rose from the table, and hid herself behind the hangings, in order to have the last word, and be able to repair, as far as possible, any mischief the old woman might do. In the meanwhile the Fairies began to endow the

Princess. The youngest, as her gift, decreed that she should be the most beautiful person in the world ; the next Fairy, that she should have an amiable mind ; the third, that she should evince the most admirable grace in all she did ; the fourth, that she should dance to perfection ; the fifth, that she should sing like a nightingale ; and the sixth that she should play on an instrument in the most exquisite manner possible. The turn of the old Fairy having arrived, she declared that the Princess should pierce her hand with a spindle, and die of the wound. This terrible fate made all the company tremble and weep.

At this moment the young Fairy issued from behind the tapestry, and said, "Comfort yourself, King and Queen : your daughter shall not die of it. The Princess will pierce her hand with a spindle, but, instead of dying, she will only fall into a deep slumber, which will last one hundred years, at the end of which a King's son will come to wake her."

The King, in hope of avoiding the misfortune predicted by the old Fairy, immediately caused an edict to be published, by which he forbade any one to spin with a spindle, or to have spindles in their possession, under pain of death.

At the end of sixteen years it happened that the Princess, while running one day about the castle, came to the top of a tower, and entered a little garret, where an old woman was sitting by herself, spinning with her distaff and spindle. This good woman had never heard of the King's edict about the spindles.

"What are you doing there ?" asked the Princess.

" I am spinning, my fair child," answered the old woman, who did not know her.

"Oh, how pretty it is !" rejoined the Princess. "How

do you do it?   Give it to me, that I may see if I can do it
as well."

She had no sooner taken hold of the spindle, than she
pierced her hand with the point of it, and fainted away.
The good old woman, very much frightened, called for help.
The King, who had run upstairs at the noise, then remembered the prediction of the Fairies, and wisely concluding
that this must have occurred as the Fairies said it would,
had the Princess conveyed into the finest apartment in the
palace, and placed on a bed of gold and silver embroidery.
Her eyes were closed, but they could hear her breathe
softly, which showed that she was not dead.   The King
commanded them to let her sleep in peace until the hour
arrived for her waking.

The good Fairy who had saved her life was in the kingdom of Mataquin, twelve thousand leagues off, when the
Princess met with her accident; but she was informed of it
instantly by a little dwarf, who had a pair of seven-league
boots, which enabled him to take seven leagues at a stride.
The Fairy set out at once, and an hour afterwards they saw
her arrive in a fiery chariot, drawn by dragons.   The King
advanced to hand her out.   She approved of all he had
done; but, as she had great foresight, she considered that
when the Princess awoke, she would feel very strange at
finding herself all alone in that old castle; so this is what
the Fairy did.   She touched with her wand everybody that
was in the castle (except the King and Queen): governesses,
maids of honour, women of the bedchamber, gentlemen,
officers, stewards, cooks, scullions, boys, guards, porters,
pages, and footmen; she touched also the horses that were
in the stables, with their grooms, the great mastiffs in the

courtyard, and little Dash, the tiny dog of the Princess, that was on the bed. beside her. As soon as she had touched them, they all fell asleep, not to wake again until the time arrived for their mistress to do so, in order that they might be all ready to attend upon her when she should want them. Even the spits that had been put down to the fire, laden with partridges and pheasants, went to sleep, and the fire itself also.

All this was done in a moment; the Fairies never lost much time over their work. After which, the King and Queen, having kissed their dear daughter without waking her, quitted the castle, and issued a proclamation forbidding any person whomsover to approach it. But in a quarter of an hour the Fairy caused to grow up around the park so great a quantity of trees, large and small, and of brambles and thorns, that neither man nor beast could get through them, so that nothing more was to be seen than the tops of the castle turrets.

At the end of a hundred years, the son of the King at that time upon the throne, who was of a different family to that of the sleeping Princess, having been hunting in the neighbourhood, inquired what towers they were he saw above the trees of a very thick wood. Each person answered him according to the story he had heard. Some said that it was an old haunted castle. The more general opinion was that it was the abode of an ogre.

The Prince did not know what to believe about it, when an old peasant spoke in his turn, and said to him, "Prince, it is more than fifty years ago since I heard my father say that there was in that castle the most beautiful Princess that ever was seen. That she was to sleep for a hundred years,

230

and would be awakened by a King's son, for whom she was reserved."

The young Prince, at these words, felt himself all on fire. He believed, without doubt, that he was destined to accomplish this famous adventure, and resolved to see what would come of it.

Scarcely had he approached the wood, when all those great trees, all those brambles and thorns, made way of their own accord for him to pass. He walked towards the castle, which he saw at the end of a long avenue he had entered, and what rather surprised him was, that he found none of his people had been able to follow him, the trees having closed up again as soon as he had passed.

He entered a large forecourt, where everything he saw was enough to freeze his blood with terror. A frightful silence reigned around. Nothing was to be seen but the bodies of men and animals stretched out apparently lifeless. But he soon found, by the shining noses and red faces of the porters, that they were only asleep ; and their goblets, in which were still left a few drops of wine, proved that they had dozed off while drinking. He traversed several apartments, with ladies and gentlemen, all asleep, some standing, others seated. He entered a chamber covered with gold, and saw on a bed, the curtains of which were open on each side, the most lovely sight he had ever looked upon—a charming Princess, who seemed to be about fifteen or sixteen. He approached, trembling and admiring, and knelt down beside her. At that moment, the spell being broken, the Princess awoke, and gazing upon the Prince with more tenderness than a first sight of him seemed to authorize, " Is it you, Prince ? " said she ; " you have been long waited for."

The Prince, delighted at these words, and still more by the tone in which they were spoken, knew not how to express to her his joy and gratitude. He assured her he loved her better than himself. His language was not very plain, but it pleased the more. The Princess had had time enough to consider what she should say to him; for during her long nap the good Fairy had given her the pleasure of very agreeable dreams. In short, they talked for four hours without having said half of what they had to say to each other.

In the meanwhile, all the palace had been roused at the same time as the Princess. Everybody remembered their duty, and, as they were not all in love, they were dying with hunger. The lady-in-waiting, as hungry as any of them, became impatient, and announced loudly to the Princess that the meat was on the table. The Prince assisted the Princess to rise: she was full dressed, and most magnificently, but he took care not to hint to her that she was attired like his grandmother. She looked, however, not a morsel less lovely.

They passed into a hall of mirrors, in which they supped, attended by the officers of the Princess. The violins and hautboys played old but excellent pieces of music, notwithstanding it was a hundred years since they had been performed by anybody; and after supper the Grand Almoner married the royal lovers in the chapel of the castle.

THE THREE BEARS.

———o———

In a far-off country there was once a little girl, who was called Silver-Locks, because her curly hair shone so very brightly. But she was not so good as she was pretty, for she was a sad romp, and so restless that she could not be kept quiet at home, and would often run out when she was told not to do so.

One day she started off into a wood, to gather wild flowers and to chase butterflies. She ran here, and she ran there, and went so far, at last, that she found herself in quite a lonely place, and there she saw a snug little house, in which three bears lived; but they were not then at home.

The door and the parlour window being open, Silver-Locks peeped in, and soon found the place

236

was empty; so the saucy puss made up her mind to go in boldly, and look all about the place, little thinking what sort of folks lived there.

Now the three bears had gone out to take a walk, a little while before this. The biggest of them was the Papa Bear, who had a very rough coat, and was named Mr. Bruin. The next bear in size was his wife, called Mammy Muff, from her smooth skin; and the smallest of the three was their little darling, Tiny.

Before going out, Mammy Muff put the nice soup she had made for dinner on a great chest in the parlour to cool; as they were very hungry, they meant to be back in a short time.

When Silver-Locks went into the house, she soon found by the smell that something nice had been cooked.

On going into the parlour, sure enough she saw there three jars smoking away: the first a very large

one, for Mr. Bruin; the next of middling size for Mammy Muff; and the smallest of all was Tiny's jar; and in each of them was a wooden spoon.

The little busybody now went to work tasting the soup in each jar by turns; but she found the soup in the smallest jar the nicest to her taste.

Silver-Locks was now in high glee, and thought to enjoy herself, hungry as she was, by eating up all the soup in the little jar. But she was too weary to be standing all the time, so she looked about for a seat.

There were three chairs in the parlour, a very large one for Mr. Bruin, another of middling size for Mammy Muff, and a nice little chair for Tiny. The little girl tried them all in turn: she found that the smallest suited her best, and down she sat, and began to eat her soup with great relish.

When Silver-Locks had nearly eaten up all poor Tiny's soup, she began to rock herself to and fro in

240

his little chair : she had often been punished for this naughty trick, but without effect. While she was indulging this silly whim, out came the rush bottom of the chair, and she and the soup-jar rolled on the floor. But she did not mind this at all, thinking it was fine fun.

She now thought she would go upstairs, and see all that was to be seen ; and there we will leave her for the present.

When the three bears came back, they found that some one had been there.

"WHO HAS BEEN TO MY SOUP?" roared out Mr. Bruin, in a loud angry voice.

"AND WHO HAS BEEN TO MY SOUP?" said Mammy Muff, with a low growl.

Then poor Tiny cried, "*Somebody has been to my soup, and eaten it all up!*"

Then said the big bear, fiercely, "WHO HAS MOVED MY CHAIR ABOUT?"

Mammy Muff, too, said, "WHO HAS MOVED MY CHAIR ABOUT?"

Then Tiny cried pitifully, "*Somebody has sat in my chair, and broken it!*"

In the room upstairs there were three beds: the largest was Mr. Bruin's bed; the next was Mammy Muff's; and the smallest of the three was Tiny's bed.

Silver-Locks tried them all, but she found the little one the most comfortable; and as she was very sleepy, she crept into it, and fell fast asleep.

The three bears, thinking that somebody was in the house, came upstairs to look, and found their beds had been disturbed, and they all, in angry voices, asked who had dared to do it.

Silver-Locks did not hear the gruff voices of Mr. and Mrs. Bruin, but the sharp squeak of Master Tiny's voice aroused her from her slumber.

"*Somebody has disturbed my bed!*" cried he; and

in a moment after he added, "*and here she is !*" looking at the same time as fierce as a little bear who had lost his dinner could do.

The little girl was now almost frightened to death, especially when she saw at the other end of the room two larger bears, in a terrible rage. Luckily for her, there was an open window close to Tiny's bed, and seeing this, she jumped out of bed in a moment, and then took a spring, and escaped out of the window, falling on some soft grass below.

The three bears came to the open window, and stared wildly at her, so she soon got up, and ran as fast as she could until she got safe home again.

Here she was properly punished for her wilful behaviour, besides the great fright she suffered from the savage looks and angry growling of the three bears.

TINY CAUGHT AT HER LOOKING-GLASS.

246

TINY AND HER VANITY;

OR, SELF-OPINION.

TINY was the smallest child you can imagine; and that was the cause of her being called Tiny, which means smaller than small. You could hardly get your thumb into her shoe, and her frock was a perfect marvel; why, a good-sized wax doll would have been bigger than Tiny. Her stockings were knit at home by her mother, for no shopkeeper dealt in such little things. So Tiny was she very justly called, until her proper name was quite forgotten. Indeed, I never knew it; but it is not of much consequence, as this story has to do with her mind and not with her name, one being very different from the other; for, though her name was small, her vanity was very great. She thought herself the handsomest girl in the town: no one else could be at all equal to her.

"Such a face as mine," she would say to herself, "is not to be met with anywhere; my bright and soft blue eyes, my lips so red, my dimpled cheek ruddy with health, and above all, my fair noble brow, over which curl the auburn ringlets worth their weight in diamonds! Where is the girl to compare with me?"

She would spend a long time every day before a looking-glass, putting her hair in vairous forms and fashions, placing herself in all sorts of attitudes, and smiling, pouting, frowning; in fact, she was never tired of admiring herself.

She was not only vain of herself, but she treated every one else with disdain and rudeness, thinking them quite beneath her notice. She often amused herself in watching the little girls go by the window, and in finding fault with them. "Oh, what hands that girl has!" "Look at that turn-up nose!" "Did you ever see such a way of walking?" "I should not like to have such rat's-tails on my head as that girl has!" Such were the remarks she used to make about passers-by. The effect of all this was that there were a good many persons who did not like her, for no one likes those who are haughty and rude.

Most of this was the fault of her mother, who used to spend

much time in dressing her and making her look as pretty as she could. Her mother, too, was so foolish as to be always praising Tiny, and agreeing with the ill-natured things she said.

When she was dressed, she marched up and down before the other cottagers' doors, to let them admire her; and they, with very good nature, would exclaim, "Oh, how beautiful to be sure! What beautiful eyes! What lovely hair! She really is a perfect little beauty!" Now, all this Tiny believed, and her vanity became greater than ever.

One morning, not content with this, she went to admire herself in the glassy surface of a brook that was near. As she stood, quite charmed with her figure, which she saw in the water, she was startled by a voice crying "Good morning, Great Vanity!"

She looked up and beheld a beautiful lady, with bright wings, on the opposite bank, and with her a frightful little dwarf, and both lady and dwarf were laughing at her.

"No doubt you think yourself perfect," continued the lady, as soon as she could stop laughing, "ay, and very wonderful, too, in your beautiful form; but, little creature, there are many more beautiful and perfect things that you tread under your small foot. If you remain through life the same vain creature, you will be a trouble to yourself and a laughingstock to other people. But I will venture to give you a lesson, which I hope will help you to become wiser, and save you from much pain. I will present you with a pair of wings, to aid you in your search after the truth. They will only last you a few hours, but by their means you will be able to see that there is vanity in others as well as in yourself, and so judge how very silly it is."

Tiny started as she felt her wings spring from her shoulders and raise her from the earth. Although alarmed at her flight, she soon began to enjoy the new and pleasing sensation of being borne through the air. She closed her wings and settled down amidst some beautiful wild flowers, close to a large *barn owl*, who had lost his way in the daylight.

"What are you?" said he in a husky voice, as he tried to make her out in the blinding sunshine.

"Please, sir," replied she, "I am a little girl."

"Oh, dear, only a little girl! Ah!" said he, "I thought you were a bird. Why, you've surely got wings!"

"Yes, sir, I have wings," said she, timidly, on finding how little the owl thought of a little girl; "a good Fairy gave them to me, that I might see the world."

"Ha! ha! ha!" laughed the owl; "see the world, indeed! What's the wisdom of that? Why, I, who live in a barn almost all my life, am the wisest of birds!"

"Oh, indeed, are you, sir?" said Tiny, eagerly, "perhaps you will tell me something of what you know; then I shall be wiser."

"Well!" said the owl, shutting his eyes, as if he were looking inside his head for his wisdom, "I don't know about that. I don't much desire to be a schoolmaster, but I can easily tell you what I know: that is, I know that I am wise, as everybody says so; and I believe so, because the cleverest of people say that I am the wisest of birds; so you may rest content with that, and go on, and

let me find my way back to the barn." With that he looked wiser than ever, chuckling over his own fun.

"What a vain, stupid old thing!" said Tiny, as the owl went hopping on his way. "Well! I've learnt nothing from him."

As she fluttered in a neighbouring wood, she was rather startled at seeing a gigantic *kangaroo*, who was springing forward by the help of his long, strong tail. She watched him cautiously. Whilst doing so a large blue *stork* came out from a damp, reedy corner, and walked up to the kangaroo.

"Oh! there you are, Mr. Jumper, are you?" said the stork; "why, what an enormous tail you've got! Why don't you carry it properly, and not make a leg of it? By-the-bye, are those wretched little things your fore-legs? I mean those little bits hanging down in front."

"Impudent bird!" replied the kangaroo, with a look of contempt, "do you pretend to make fun of my perfect and beautiful form, which is in every way a better one than that of any other beast? Where is the animal that can leap as far as I can? My beautiful tail, which is in itself a wonder, for it helps me to· perform my immense leaps; and my charming little fore-legs, which are so fit for the use to which I put them! Bah! go back, silliest of birds, to the swamp, where no one can see you, and hide those long sticks of legs, that lift you up so high in the world and make your ugliness to be seen farther off. If you can find water enough near at hand, go and use it as a looking-glass, and look at your ugly self, and blush, if you can through your feathers, when you see what a contrast there is between yourself and such a perfect creature as I am." Without waiting a moment for the stork's reply, he bounded into the wood with a savage cry.

"Well!" said Tiny, when the stork flew off, "that's pretty well on both sides. They are ready to admire themselves and to despise each other. Each thinks himself the most beautiful animal in the world, and yet what ugly things they both are."

Tiny flew on, and found herself close by the trunk of a large spreading tree, upon a branch of which was perched a beautiful Malabar *squirrel*, quite at his ease, cracking nuts and enjoying the warm sunshine.

"I wonder whether he can speak," thought Tiny; "but I dare say he can, for he has a very sharp look."

She had hardly thought this, when at her feet she saw the funniest little *guinea-pig* pop out of the underwood, snuffing his way in the most cautious manner. The squirrel stopped cracking his nuts, and, throwing down some shells upon the guinea-pig, called out in a loud voice,

"Hallo, there, you little wretch! where are you going? what do you call yourself? and pray, if it be not rude, will you allow me to inquire what has become of your tail?"

The guinea-pig looked round with a puzzled air, to find out where these polite questions came from. At last he saw the squirrel, and with a very humble air replied, "If you please, my very good sir, I don't remember being ever troubled with a tail."

"What do you mean by that?" said the squirrel, in a huff. And down he jumped, and stood right in front of the pig.

"What I mean," replied the pig, not at all afraid, "is that I should find a cumbrous brush like yours a great deal of trouble and very much in the way, and, I think, also dangerous ; for you, foolish nutcracker, would be much safer if you did not flourish that tail about so much, in your vanity, for it is the means of your being found out by the hunter, and is, therefore, I repeat, a great evil to you. You would live much longer had you a tail much shorter. Cannot you have it cut off ? it is as useless as it is ugly ; so I wish you a good morning, and less vanity."

The pig vanished into the earth, and the squirrel sprang into the tree to hide himself.

Tiny fluttered on, quite amused with the sharp reply of the stupid-looking pig. Presently a handsome *butterfly* passed close to her, stopped in his flight, wondering at her unusual appearance, and settled close to where Tiny was.

"Good morning, my dear," said he, politely. "'Pon my honour, you quite puzzled me at first. I thought you might be some butter-fly of my acquaintance; but I found I had made a mistake when I saw how thick your legs were, and how very clumsy your form was; but still, even though you are not at all beautiful, I am glad to see you, so let us have a chat, but don't tread upon me with your great feet."

Tiny, very far from pleased at being invited in this insulting way, was about to reply, when a *snail* crawled on to the scene.

"Dear me," said the butterfly, "here is a horrid thing! Poor creature! doomed to crawl the earth with that ugly shell on its back."

"Whom are you pitying, trifler?" said the snail. "Is it for you to insult a creature like me because you have a fine coat on your back, when you were but yesterday a poor grub, very much more ugly than anything else that I can at this moment recollect? You, who have so short a life—which to be sure is long enough to do no-thing in—to talk of pity! You, an outcast, without a home that you can call your own, for you will lodge anywhere, to talk to a householder like me! Go on with you, and rob every flower that is unwise enough to take you in."

"Low creature," said the butterfly, "I shall spoil the beauty of my wings by staying near you, to be covered by your offensive slime." So saying, after flying about to show off the colours on its wings, it shot out into the broad sunshine.

"Oh, oh!" said Tiny, as she flew on her way, "there I think vanity was properly schooled."

Soon the sun became burning hot, and Tiny found herself on some scorching sands, where lay an enormous black *tortoise*. So still was it that at first she supposed it to be a great black stone; but a slight movement of the head showed that it was alive. As she stood gazing at it, a long shadow fell over it, which, upon look-ing up, she saw was caused by the approach of a tall *giraffe*.

"Well, my little dear," said he, "are you looking upon that most miserable being, that might as well be a stone, which it has all the appearance of? I don't think it has moved on its way for months, poor lump of dullness! To be sure, it cannot be expected," con-tinued he, arching his long neck with much pride, "that everything can be made handsome, graceful, like me—oh, dear, dear, no! I can

reach with my mouth the leaves at the very top of a tree, can see danger afar off, and can run so swiftly that no animal can overtake me. I cannot help pitying such a creature as this at my feet, who seems as if he had dropped on the sands without legs to carry him anywhere."

The tortoise moved his head, and casting up his eyes, said in a slow and solemn manner to the giraffe,

"Long-legged, long-necked, useless, ungraceful animal! how painful is it to hear a thing of a few short years of life talk about its being better than others! My legs are not so long but that I can put them away safely, that no one may tread on my toes; my neck is long enough to enable me to look out of my front door,

and short enough to be packed inside at the approach of danger. No weight can crush me, no animal can hurt me. Of what use would long legs be to me, when I never need run away? and my life is so long that I was in the world fifty years before your grand-father, whose bones are bleaching upon the sands of the desert. So let your long legs take you away, that your vanity may not offend me any more."

After hearing this conversation, Tiny said to herself,

"How all the animals praise themselves, and find fault with one another in this part of the world! I wonder whether it is the same elsewhere; I must go and see."

Distance being nothing to Tiny now that she had wings, she flew off to another part of the world, where the air was cooler. Here she stood upon the rocks, where an old *penguin* was admiring the rolling of the waves as they washed his feet.

"A nice cool breeze here," said Tiny.

"Very nice and refreshing," replied the penguin. And to show its effects, he flapped his little wings, that looked as if made of leather. "This place," continued he, "is the most healthy and pleasant in the world."

"Indeed!" said Tiny, not knowing what to say.

"Don't waste your time, little girl, in such bad company," screamed an *eagle* from a cliff close by. "That half-bird, half-fish, talks in the silliest way, like a relation of his, the booby. He is a disgrace to the family of birds. In the first place, he walks upright, like a man; in the second place, has nothing which he can call a wing. Now, I am the king of birds. I can fly nearer the sun than any other bird; I can carry a lamb entire to my nest at the top of the mountain, where none can follow. I can talk to you in a kingly way; so fly up here, that I may honour you with a few minutes' chat, that will instruct and please you."

"Stop where you are, my child," said the penguin. "I may be humble and ugly, as that king of birds in the most unkingly manner observes, but I am honest, which he is not; for he, who disgraces the name of king, is a plunderer and robber, a bird of prey, without kindness and pity, who stains himself with innocent blood, and rejoices in a cruel nature."

"Say you so, most fishy of birds?" screamed the eagle, making a tremendous swoop to seize the penguin in his claws. But the penguin knew his revengeful nature, and sought safety beneath the wave of the sea, above which the eagle hovered in wide circles, in hopes of glutting his revenge. But the penguin did not appear, so the savage eagle had to return home without punishing what he took as an insult to his royal dignity.

Tiny shuddered at the screams of the fierce eagle, and flew on her way until she rested herself in a beautiful flowery vale, where her eyes were attracted by myriads of lovely blossoms, that scented the air around them. A superb *arum lily* reared its snow-white crest and golden crown high above her head. She could but admire its graceful queen-like form. As she drew nearer, she beheld bright drops of water hanging from its leaves, that shone and sparkled like jewels ere they fell.

"Little child," said the lily, in a proud and haughty tone,

"approach! I am not timid. I was born to be admired; it is my lot to be the delight of all who look upon me."

Tiny went close to the lily, and modestly attempted to inhale the odour of the beautiful flower, but started back on finding that the scent that came from it was acrid and unpleasant, and to get rid of it she plucked a few *violets* that grew beneath her feet.

"Thank you, dear child," said the violets, "for placing us in your bosom without any of our self-praise. Let it be ever thus with you; never despise the humble when you are in company with the aspiring and proud. Look upon yonder stately lily, whose look claims our attention and regard, whilst it has no inward worth to

gain our love. The more we know of it, the less we like it. Those
dew-drops that hang like bright jewels from its leaves are but, in
truth, tears which it sheds, because its flowers can only be admired
at a distance, on account of their unpleasant smell. To appear
good and not to be good will never secure esteem or happiness."
Tiny pressed the violets to her bosom for their sweet lesson,
and went on her way, which brought her into a beautiful garden,
where a handsome *cat* was enjoying herself in state on a terrace
walk.

"Puss! Puss!" said Tiny, stroking the sleeping beauty, "good
morning to you."

"Oh! good morning: how are you?" replied Puss. "I really did not see you; for I was half asleep, after being up half the night at a mouse party."

"Indeed!" said Tiny: "was it amusing?"

"To *me*," said the cat, slily, with a very slight wink; "not to them."

"Ah! I understand," said Tiny. "Oh! Puss! Puss!"

"Did you call me?" said a pert young *hare*, popping out from beneath a plant with large leaves that had concealed her.

"You!" said the cat, looking down with contempt; "are you Puss?"

"Yes, I am called Puss by the most respectable people," sharply replied the hare.

"You are a gipsy," replied the cat, "and live in a mud house ; you are nothing like a cat, except in your whiskers, which you have had the impudence to copy from mine. Where is your tail, friend ? Cat, indeed !"

"Tail ! pooh !" said the hare ; "that would be of very little use to me. Of what use is your tail to you, except to show when you are angry ? But look at my fine long ears : something like ears, mine are. Pray, where are yours ? I can scarcely see them."

The cat did not deign to reply, but rubbed her nose with her paw.

"You talk to me," said the hare, " I, who am sought after by the very highest people in the neighbourhood, and am at most of their tables ! I live at large on my own estate, quite as good a country gentleman as any of them. I have a domain of my own underground, whilst you are a short-eared, long-tailed servant, living upon mice and anything you can catch ; and not good for any known dish when you are dead. Ha ! ha ! ha ! Puss, indeed ! You are a mouse-trap."

So saying, he struck his foot upon the ground, and trotted away. The cat muttered to herself, "fellow !"

"Croak ! croak !" went a *frog* close by, which attracted Tiny to the spot. There he sat, upon a little bank, enjoying the warmth of the sun, and croaking as loud as he could. As she was looking at him, a *fish*, with silver scales and glittering eyes, popped his nose out of the water, and looked to see where the harsh sound came from.

"I wish to goodness, you dreadful thing, you would cease that horrid noise. I can't get my little ones to sleep for it."

"Hold your tongue !" said the frog, carelessly playing with a bulrush. "If you bother me about your young ones, you shan't remain in my pond."

"Your pond, indeed, reptile !" said the proud fish, "why don't you come and live in it, then ? But, no ; you can't remain in it long: it is too fine for you, muddy monster. Then see how gracefully I can swim, but every one laughs at your hopping and jumping."

"Don't be in a passion, my good fish," said the frog. "If you were a gentleman you would come out here and talk ; but you have nothing to stand upon, so I pity you. You are an imperfect thing, and therefore beneath the notice of one who stands upon his own land. You are welcome to call the pond yours, for I only do my washing there."

The fish swam away without replying to this rude remark.

Again Tiny's flight took her to the sea-shore, where she was rather startled by the appearance of a large *crab*, who was hurrying along sideways, as if upon some important business. But something caught him by the toe and threw him over. On getting up again, he saw that it was an *oyster* washed up to the edge of the tide.

"Stupidest of fish," exclaimed the crab, in a passion, "could you not get out of the way when you saw me coming? I declare that you have caused me to hurt one of my claws dreadfully."

The oyster, opening his shell very slowly to reply, said, "Pray, sir, who may you be?

" Don't you see I am a splendid crab ? " replied he.

" Oh ! I see," said the oyster; " a shell-fish ! one of us ! "

" One of us ! " replied the crab, in scorn. " One of us ! Do you pretend to class yourself with me ?—a beautiful structure, with claws that can nip like a pair of pincers ; with eyes that can see, and armour of the most perfect make ; the very best and the most prized of shell-fish ; and to be classed after all with a thing like you ! a lump ! a stone ! washed about by the sea, without the power of guiding yourself ; and nothing more, the better part of your time, than a bit of stone clinging to a rock."

Ha ! ha ! ha ! " laughed the oyster. " You stupid, vain thing ! I really cannot help laughing at you. Why, with all your claws, both thick and thin, you can only scramble sideways, and cannot even walk straight. Ha ! ha ! ha ! " laughed the oyster, as he snapped his shell.

The crab popped into the water without a word.

Tiny turned from the sea and flew towards the fields, where she soon got into the company of a fine *grasshopper*, whose golden eyes glistened amidst the grass.

" How d' ye do, dear ? " chirped he ; " I am glad to see you, for I have been bored to death with this stupid *mole*." As he spoke, he pointed out to Tiny the mole's nose just peeping out of his hill.

" You see," said he, " instead of being like me, dressed in the splendid green livery of the fields, and being beautifully gilded, he is but a poor, buried know-nothing, and therefore, of course, only very dull company, and a mere clod."

" If coats and gilding were of any use, I would say that your value was indeed great," said the mole ; " but as you do nothing but chirp, I cannot give you the credit you desire, and must, therefore, consider myself the better of the two ; for I devour the vermin that would eat up all the corn and destroy the grass that shelters you ; so that, although buried, I am useful to others, and am greatly valued by all those who know me."

" Honesty reproving vanity again," thought Tiny, as she flew away, leaving the mole to burrow in the ground, and the other to hop and chirp.

" Where are you flying so fast ? " said a little blue *titmouse*, as he fluttered on the trunk of a tree.

" I am making haste to see as much as I can," said Tiny, " for my wings leave me at sunset."

" Well, then, the sun is now setting," said he, " and I have saved you a fall."

As he spoke, Tiny was grieved to see her wings on the ground. " Thank you, good little bird," said Tiny, in a sorrowful voice ; " but how am I to get home ? "

" Take courage," said the titmouse ; " the good Fairy will still protect you, so don't be afraid." Saying this, he flew away.

As she stood, almost weeping, a large *ostrich* strutted up to her, proudly spreading out his beautiful feathers.

" Little girl," said he, " perhaps you can decide between me and that ugly bird in yonder tree which is the prettier."

" Ugly bird, indeed ! " said a queer *toucan,* as he snapped his beak, which was nearly as large as himself. " I should like to know

where you will see so foolish a bird as the ostrich, whose body is covered with such an abundance of feathers, while his legs are left bare, and his wings tempt his enemies to destroy him, but have not power to carry him out of danger.   Why, my beautiful beak alone is worth a thousand times more than his whole body."

"Well, I am content to leave the little girl to decide," said the ostrich.

Tiny, who really admired the beautiful ostrich, and could hardly refrain from laughing outright at the toucan, found sufficient courage at last to say,

"Well, I think, ostrich, that you are much the handsomer of the two."

The toucan flew away in disgust, and the ostrich, who was exceedingly well pleased with what Tiny had said, turned proudly to the little child, and said,

"Where are you going, little maid?"

"Oh, many, many miles," said she, "and I much fear that I shall never get home, since I have flown about for so long a time hither and thither."

"Get up on my back," said the ostrich, stooping down, so that she might nestle between his wings, where she was no sooner

snugly placed, than he started and sped like the wind across the
hills, and the valleys, and the sands, until he arrived at the sea-
shore.   Here he stopped, unable, of course, to go farther with his
little charge.

"Now, good ostrich, what am I to do?" said Tiny.

"Wait a bit," said he; "here comes a beautiful *nautilus*, who, I
dare say, will take you swiftly and carefully across the sea."

The nautilus very lightly skimmed over the waves until he
touched the sand.

"Step in, little girl," said he, "and I will bear you safely over the
waters to your home, for so the good Fairy has commanded me."

Tiny did not hesitate a moment, but stepped into the shell, which bore her lightly over the dancing foam of the sea, and before night landed her safely on the shore close to her home. As she walked towards the light shining in her cottage window, she thought how kind the Fairy had been to let her learn whilst young how foolish it is to think ourselves better, and prettier, and wiser than others. She also saw how wrong it was to laugh at others, to find fault with them, and to treat them with disdain; for they are sure to be superior to us in something. So Tiny left off gazing at herself in the looking-glass, and thought no more about her pretty face and fine figure, except to make herself clean and neat. She also ceased to make remarks against the little girls that passed her window; but, instead of this, said as much good of others as she could, and never spoke ill of them. And every one who knew Tiny began to love her, and talked no more about TINY AND HER VANITY, but spoke of TINY AND HER GOODNESS.

TOM THUMB.

———o———

MERLIN, the magician, once stopped at the cottage of a poor couple, who treated him very kindly to the best they had. He saw that they were not content with their lot, and the cottager's wife told him what it was that made them so sorrowful: they much wanted to have a son; and she added, "If it was even no bigger than his father's thumb!"

When the Queen of the Fairies heard from Merlin of this wish of the honest couple, she promised to grant it. By-and-bye they had, to their great delight, a little son, and sure enough he was no bigger than a large thumb, and was called, accordingly, TOM THUMB; and, owing to his very small size, he was always getting into scrapes.

When he was old enough to play with the boys for cherry-stones, and had lost all his own, he used to creep into the other boys' bags, fill his pockets, and come out again to play. But one day as he was getting out of a bag of cherry-stones, the boy to whom it belonged chanced to see him.

"Ah, ah! my little Tom Thumb!" said the boy, "have I caught you at your bad tricks at last? now I will pay you off for thieving."

Then drawing the string tight round his neck, and shaking the bag heartily, the cherry-stones bruised Tom's limbs and body sadly, which made him beg to be let out and promise never to be guilty of such doings any more.

Shortly afterwards, Tom's mother was making a batter pudding, and, that he might see how she mixed it, he climbed up to the edge of the bowl; but his foot happening to slip, he fell over head and ears into the batter, and his mother not observing him, stirred him into the pudding, and popped it all into the pot to boil. The hot water made Tom kick and struggle; and his mother seeing the pudding jump up and down in such a furious manner, thought it was bewitched; a tinker was coming by just at the time, so she quickly gave him the pudding, and he put it into his bag and walked away.

As soon as Tom could get the batter out of his mouth, he began to cry aloud; this so frightened the poor tinker, that he flung the pudding over the hedge, and ran away from it as fast as he could. The pudding being broken to pieces by the fall, Tom was released, and walked home to his mother, who gave him a kiss and put him to bed; and much pleased was she at finding him again.

Tom Thumb's mother once took him with her when she went to milk the cow, and it being a very windy day, she tied him with a needleful of thread to a thistle, that he might not be blown away. The cow, liking his oak-leaf hat, took him and the thistle up at one mouthful. While the cow was chewing the thistle, Tom, terrified at her great teeth, which seemed ready to crush him to pieces, cried out, "Mother, mother!" as loud as he could bawl. His mother began to cry and wring her hands; but the cow, surprised at such odd noises in her throat, opened her mouth and let him drop out. His mother then clapped him into her apron, and ran home with him.

Tom's father made him a whip of a barley straw to drive

the cattle with, and being one day in the field, Tom slipped into a deep furrow. A raven flying over, picked him up with a grain of corn, and flew with him to the top of a giant's castle, by the sea-side, where he left him. Old Grumbo, the giant, came out soon afterwards to walk upon his terrace, and Tom, frightened out of his wits, managed to creep up his sleeve. Tom's motions made the giant feel very uncomfortable, and with a jerk of the arm he threw him into the sea. A great fish then swallowed him. This fish was soon after caught, and sent as a present to the King. When it was cut open, everybody was delighted with little Tom Thumb, who was found inside. The King made him his dwarf; he became the favourite of the whole Court, and by his merry pranks often amused the Queen and the Knights of the Round Table.

The King, when he rode out, frequently took Tom in his hand; and, if a shower of rain came on, the tiny dwarf used to creep into the King's waistcoat-pocket, and sleep till the rain was over. One day the King asked him about his parents; and when Tom informed his Majesty they were very poor people, the King told him he should pay them a visit, and take with him as much money as he could carry. Tom got a little purse, and putting a threepenny-piece into it, with much difficulty got it upon his back, and after travelling two days and nights, arrived at his father's house. His mother met him at the door almost tired to death, he having travelled forty-eight hours without resting. They placed him in a walnut-shell by the fireside, and feasted him for three days upon a hazel-nut.

Tom soon got well, and his mother took him in her hand, and carried him back to King Arthur's Court; there

Tom entertained the King and Queen, and nobility, at tilts and tournaments, at which he exerted himself so much, that he brought on a fit of sickness, and his life was despaired of.

At this juncture the Queen of the Fairies came in a chariot drawn by flying mice, and placing Tom by her side, she drove through the air without stopping till they arrived at her palace. After restoring him to health, and per-mitting him to enjoy all the gay diversions of Fairyland, the Queen commanded a fair wind, and placing Tom before it, blew him straight back to the Court of King Arthur. But just as Tom should have alighted in the courtyard of the palace, the cook happened to pass along with the King's great bowl of his favourite dish of furmenty, and poor Tom Thumb fell plump into the middle of it, and splashed the hot furmenty into the cook's eyes. Down went the bowl.

"Oh, dear! oh, dear!" cried Tom.

"Murder! murder!" bellowed the cook; and away went the King's nice furmenty into the kennel.

The cook was a red-faced, cross fellow, and declared to the King that Tom had done it out of some evil design so he was taken up, tried for high treason, and sentenced to be beheaded. When the Judge delivered this dreadful sentence, it happened that a miller was standing by with his mouth wide open, so Tom took a good spring, and jumped down his throat, unperceived by all in the Court of Justice, even by the miller himself.

As Tom could not be found, the Court broke up, and away went the miller to his mill. But Tom did not leave him long at rest; he began to roll and tumble about, so that the miller thought himself bewitched, and sent for a

doctor. When the doctor came Tom began to dance and sing; the doctor was as much frightened as the miller, and sent in great haste for five more doctors.

While all these were talking about the disorder in a very tedious style, the miller began to yawn, and Tom, taking the opportunity, made another bold jump, and alighted on his feet in the middle of the table. The miller, provoked to be thus tormented by such a little creature, fell into a great passion, caught hold of Tom, and threw him out of the window into the river. A large salmon swimming by, snapped him up in a moment, as he would a fly.

The salmon was soon caught and sold in the market to the steward of a great lord, who made a present of it to the King. When the cook cut open the salmon, he found poor Tom inside, and ran with him directly to the King; but the King, being busy with state affairs, desired that he might be brought another day.

The cook was resolved to keep him safely this time, as he had so lately given him the slip, so clapped him into a mouse-trap. There he was shut up for a whole week, when the King sent for him, forgave him for throwing down the furmenty, and ordered him new clothes, gave him a spirited mouse for a hunter, and knighted him.

As they were riding by a farm-house one day, a cat jumped from behind the door, seized the mouse and little Tom, ran off with them both, and was just going to devour the mouse, when Tom boldly drew his sword and attacked the cat with great spirit. The King and his nobles seeing Tom in danger, went to his assistance, and one of the lords saved him just in time.

The King ordered a little chair to be made, that Tom

278

might sit on his table. He also gave him a coach drawn by six small mice. This made the Queen angry, because she had not a new coach too; therefore, to ruin Tom, she complained to the King that he had behaved very insolently to her. The King, in a rage, then sent for him. Tom, to escape his fury, crept into a large empty snail-shell, and there lay till he was almost starved; when, peeping out of the shell, he saw a fine butterfly that had just settled on the ground. He now ventured forth, and got astride the butterfly, which took wing and mounted into the air with little Tom on his back. Away he flew from tree to tree, till at last he flew to the King's Court.

The King, Queen, and nobles, all strove to catch the butterfly, but could not. At length poor Tom, having neither bridle nor saddle, slipped from his seat, and fell into a sweet dish called white-pot, where he was found almost drowned. The Queen vowed he should be punished, and he was secured once more in a mouse-trap; when the cat seeing something stir, and supposing it to be a mouse, patted the trap about till she broke it, and set Tom at liberty.

Soon afterwards, a spider, taking poor Tom for a big fly, made a spring at him. Tom drew his sword and fought valiantly, but the spider's poisonous breath overcame him:—

> He fell dead on the ground where he late had stood,
> And the spider sucked up the last drop of his blood.

The King and his whole Court went into mourning for little Tom Thumb. They buried him under a rose-bush, and raised a nice white marble monument over his grave.

MOTHER DUCK AND HER DUCKLINGS.

THE UGLY DUCKLING.

IN a sunny spot stood an old country house, encircled by canals.
Between the wall and the water's edge there grew huge burdock-
leaves, that had shot up to such a height that a little child might
have stood upright under the tallest of them ; and this spot was as
wild as though it had been situated in the depths of a wood.   In
this snug retirement a duck was sitting on her nest to hatch her
young ; but she began to think it a wearisome task, as the little
ones seemed very backward in making their appearance ; besides,
she had few visitors, for the other ducks preferred swimming about
in the canals, instead of being at the trouble of climbing up the
slope, and then sitting under a burdock-leaf to gossip with her.

At length. one egg cracked, and then another. "Peep! peep!" cried they, as each yolk became a live thing, and popped out its head.

"Quack! quack!" said the mother; and they tried to cackle like her, while they looked all about them under the green leaves; and she allowed them to look to their hearts' content, because green is good for the eyes.

"How large the world is, to be sure!" said the young ones. And truly enough, they had rather more room than when they were still in the egg-shell.

"Do you fancy this is the whole world?" cried the mother. "Why, it reaches far away beyond the other side of the garden, down to the parson's field; though I never went to such a distance as that! But are you all there?" continued she, rising. "No, faith! you are not; for there still lies the largest egg. I wonder how long this business is to last—I really begin to grow quite tired of it!" And she sat down once more.

"Well, how are you getting on?" inquired an old duck, who came to pay her a visit.

"This egg takes a deal of hatching," answered the sitting duck: "it won't break. But just look at the others; are they not the prettiest ducklings ever seen? They are the image of their father.

"Let me look at the egg that won't break," quoth the old duck. "Take my word for it, it must be a guinea-fowl's egg. I was once

deceived in the same way, and I bestowed a deal of care and
anxiety on the youngsters, for they are afraid of water. I could

not make them take to it. I stormed and raved, but it was of **no**

use. Let's see the egg. Sure enough, it is a guinea-fowl's **egg.**

Leave it alone, and set about teaching the other children to swim."

"I'll just sit upon it a bit longer," said the duck; "for, since I have sat so long, a few days more won't make much odds."

"Please yourself," said the old duck, as she went away.

At length the large egg cracked. "Peep! peep! peep!" squeaked the youngster as he crept out. How big and ugly he

was, to be sure! The duck looked at him, saying, "Really, this is a most enormous duckling! None of the others are like him. I wonder whether he is a guinea-chick after all? Well, we shall

soon see when we get down to the water, for in he shall go, though
I push him in myself."

On the following morning the weather was most delightful, and

the sun was shining brightly on the green burdock-leaves. The
mother duck took her young brood down to the canal. Splash

into the water she went. "Quack! quack!" cried she, and forthwith one duckling after another jumped. The water closed over
their heads for a moment; but they soon rose to the surface again,
and swam about so nicely, just as if their legs paddled them about

of their own accord; and they had all taken to the water; even
the ugly grey-coated youngster swam about with the rest.

"Nay, he is no guinea-chick," said she: "only look how capitally
he uses his legs, and how steady he keeps himself—he's every inch
my own child! And really he's very pretty when one comes to

look at him attentively. Quack! quack!" added she; "now, come along, and I'll take you into high society, and introduce you to the duck-yard; but mind you keep close to me, that nobody may tread upon you; and above all, beware of the cat."

They now reached the farm-yard, where there was a great hubbub. Two families were fighting for an eel's head, which, in the end, was carried off by the cat.

"See, children, that's the way with the world!" remarked the mother of the ducklings, licking her beak, for she would have been very glad to have had the eel's head for herself. "Now move on!" said she, "and mind you cackle properly, and bow your head before that old duck yonder : she is the noblest born of them all, and is of Spanish descent, and that's why she is so dignified ; and, look ! she has a red rag tied to her leg, which is the greatest mark of distinction that can be bestowed upon a duck, as it shows an anxiety not to lose her, and that she should be recognized by both man and beast.   Now cackle—and don't turn in your toes : a well-bred duckling spreads his feet wide apart, like papa and mamma, in this sort of way.   Now bend your neck and say 'Quack!'"

The ducklings did as they were bid ; but the other ducks, after looking at them, only said aloud, " Now look ! here comes another set, as if we were not quite numerous enough already.   And, bless me ! what a queer-looking chap one of the ducklings is, to be sure! We can't put up with him !"   And one of the throng darted forward and bit him in the neck.

" Leave him alone," said the mother ; "he did no harm to any one."

" No, but he is too big and uncouth," said the biting duck, " and therefore he wants a thrashing."

" Mamma has a sweet little family," said the old duck with the rag about her leg : "they are all pretty except one, who is rather ill-favoured.   I wish mamma could polish him a bit."

" I'm afraid that will be impossible, your grace," said the mother of the ducklings.   " It's true he is not pretty, but he has a very good disposition, and swims as well or perhaps better than all the others put together.   However, he may grow prettier, and perhaps

become smaller : he remained too long in the egg-shell, and therefore his figure is not properly formed." And with this she smoothed
down the ruffled feathers of his neck, adding, "At all events, as he

is a male duck it won't matter so much. I think he 'll prove strong,
and be able to fight his way through the world."

"The other ducklings are elegant little creatures," said the old

duck. "Now, make yourself at home ; and if you should happen
to find an eel's head, you can bring it to me."

And so the family made themselves comfortable.

But the poor duckling who had been the last to creep out of his

egg-shell, and looked so ugly, was bitten, and pushed about, and made game of, not only by the ducks, but by the hens.   They all declared he was much too big ; and a guinea-fowl who fancied himself at least an emperor, because he had come into the world with spurs, now puffed himself up like a vessel in full sail, and flew at the duckling, and blustered till his head turned completely red, so that the poor little thing did not know where he could walk or stand, and was quite grieved at being so ugly that the whole farm-yard scouted him.

Nor did matters mend the next day, or the following ones, but rather grew worse and worse.   The poor duckling was hunted down by everybody.   Even his sisters were so unkind to him, that they were continually saying, " I wish the cat would run away with you, you ugly creature!" while his mother added, "I wish you had **never** been born !" And the ducks pecked at him, the hens struck **him,** and the girl who fed the poultry used to kick him.

So he ran away and flew over the palings. The little birds **in** the bushes were startled, and took wing. " That is because I am

so ugly," thought the duckling, as he closed his eyes in despair ; but presently he roused up again, and ran on farther till he came to a large marsh inhabited by wild ducks. Here he spent the whole night, and tired and sorrowful enough he was.

On the following morning, when the wild ducks rose and saw their new comrade, they said, "What sort of a creature are you?" Upon which the duckling greeted them all round as civilly as he knew how.

"You are remarkably ugly," observed the ducks; "but we don't care about that so long as you don't want to marry into our family." Poor forlorn little creature! he had truly no such thoughts in his head: all he wanted was to obtain leave to lie among the rushes and to drink a little of the marsh-water.

He remained there for two whole days, at the end of which there came two wild geese, or, more properly speaking, goslings, who were only just out of the egg-shell, and consequently were very pert.

"I say, friend," quoth they, "you are so ugly that we should have no objection to take you with us for a travelling companion. In the neighbouring marsh there dwell some sweetly pretty female geese, all of them unmarried, and who cackle most charmingly. Perhaps you may have a chance to pick up a wife amongst them, ugly as you are."

Pop! pop! sounded through the air, and the two wild goslings fell dead amongst the rushes, while the water turned as red as blood. Pop! pop! again echoed around, and whole flocks of wild geese flew up from the rushes. Again and again the same alarming noise was heard. It was a shooting party, and the sportsmen surrounded the whole marsh, while others had climbed into the branches of the trees that overshadowed the rushes. A blue mist rose in clouds

and mingled with the green leaves, and sailed far away across the
water ; a pack of dogs next flounced into the marsh.   Splash,

splash ! they went, while the reeds and rushes bent beneath them
on all sides.   What a fright they occasioned the poor duckling !

He turned away his head to hide it under his wing, when, lo ! a
tremendous-looking dog, with his tongue lolling out and his eyes
glaring fearfully, stood right before him, opening his jaws and

showing his sharp teeth, as though he would gobble up the poor duckling at a mouthful!—but splash! splash! on he went without touching him.

"Thank goodness," sighed the duckling, "I am so ugly that even a dog won't bite me."

And he lay quite still, while the shot rattled through the rushes, and pop after pop echoed through the air.

It was not till late in the day that all became quiet, but the poor youngster did not yet venture to rise, but waited several hours before he looked about him, and then hastened out of the marsh as fast as he could go. He ran across fields and meadows, till there arose such a storm that he could scarcely get on at all.

Towards evening he reached a wretched little cottage, that was
in such a tumble-down condition, that if it remained standing at

all, it could only be from not yet having made up its mind on which
side it should fall first. The tempest was now raging to such a

height, that the duckling was forced to sit down to stem the wind,
when he perceived that the door hung so loosely on one of its
hinges, that he could slip into the room through the crack, which
he accordingly did.

The inmates of the cottage were a woman, a tom-cat, and a hen.
The tom-cat, whom she called her darling, could raise his back and
purr, and he could even throw out sparks, provided he were stroked

against the grain.   The hen had small short legs, for which reason
she was called Henny Shortlegs.   She laid good eggs, and her
mistress loved her as if she had been her own child.

Next morning they perceived the little stranger, when the tom-
cat began to purr, and the hen to cluck.

"What's that?" said the woman, looking round.   Not seeing
very distinctly, she mistook the duckling for a fat duck that had
lost its way.   "Why, this is quite a prize!" added she: "I can
now get duck's eggs, unless indeed it be a male.   We must wait a
bit and see."

So the duckling was kept on trial for three weeks; but no eggs
were forthcoming.   The tom-cat and the hen were the master and
mistress of the house, and always said "We and the world," for
they fancied themselves to be the half—and by far the best half
too—of the whole universe.   The duckling thought there might
be two opinions on this point; but the hen would not admit of any
such doubts.

"Can you lay eggs?" asked she.

"No."

"Then have the goodness to hold your tongue."

And the tom-cat inquired, "Can you raise your back, or purr, or throw out sparks?"

"No."

"Then you have no business to have any opinion at all, when rational people are talking."

The duckling sat in a corner, very much out of spirits, when in came the fresh air and sunshine, which gave him such a strange longing to swim on the water, that he could not help saying so to the hen.

"What's this whim?" said she. "That comes of being idle. If

you could either lay eggs or purr, you would not indulge in such fancies."

"But it is so delightful to swim about on the water!" the duckling observed, "and to feel it close over one's head when one dives down to the bottom."

"A great pleasure indeed!" quoth the hen. "You must be crazy, surely! Only ask the cat—for he is the wisest creature I know—how he would like to swim on the water, or to dive under it. To say nothing of myself, just ask our old mistress, who is wiser than anybody else in the world, whether she'd relish swimming and feeling the waters close above her head."

"You can't understand me," said the duckling.

"We can't understand you! I should like to know who could. You don't suppose you are wiser than the tom-cat and our mistress —to say nothing of myself? Don't take these idle fancies into your head, child. I say disagreeable things, which is a mark of true friendship. Now, look to it, and mind that you either lay eggs, or learn to purr and emit sparks."

"I think I'll take my chance, and go abroad into the wide world," said the duckling.

"Do," said the hen.

And the duckling went forth, and swam on the water, and dived beneath its surface; but he was slighted by all the other animals, on account of his ugliness.

Autumn had now set in. The leaves of the forests had turned first yellow, and then brown; and the wind caught them up, and made them dance about. It began to be very cold, and the clouds looked heavy with hail and flakes of snow; while the raven sat on a hedge, crying "Caw! caw!" from sheer cold; and one began to shiver, if one merely thought about it. One evening, just as the sun was setting, there came a whole flock of beautiful large birds from a grove. The duckling had never seen any so lovely before. They were dazzlingly white, with long graceful necks: they were swans. They uttered a peculiar cry, and then spread

their magnificent wings, and away they flew from the cold country to warmer lands across the open sea. They rose so high that the ugly duckling felt a strange sensation come over him. He turned round and round in the water like a wheel, stretched his neck up into the air towards them, and uttered so loud and strange a cry, that he was frightened at it himself. Oh! never could he again forget those beautiful, happy birds; and when they were quite out of sight, he dived down to the bottom of the water, and when he once more rose to the surface, he was half beside himself. He knew not how these birds were called, nor whither they were bound; but he felt an affection for them, such as he had never yet experienced for any living creature. Nor did he even presume to envy them; for how could it ever have entered his head to wish himself endowed with their loveliness? He would have been glad enough if the ducks had merely suffered him to remain among them—poor ugly animal that he was!

And winter proved so very, very cold. The duckling was obliged to keep swimming about, for fear the water should freeze entirely; but every night the hole in which he swam grew smaller and yet

smaller. It now froze so hard that the surface of the ice cracked again; yet the duckling still paddled about, to prevent the hole from closing up. At last he was so exhausted that he lay insensible, and became ice-bound.

Early next morning a peasant came by, and seeing what had taken place, broke the ice to pieces with his wooden shoe, and carried the duckling home to his wife; so the little creature was revived once more.

The children wished to play with him; but the duckling thought they intended to hurt him, and in his fright he plunged right into a

bowl of milk, that was spirted all over the room. The woman clapped her hands, which only frightened him still more, and drove

him first into the butter-tub, then down into the meal-tub, and out again. What a scene then ensued! The woman screamed, and flung the tongs at him; the children tumbled over each other in their endeavours to catch the duckling, and laughed and shrieked. For-

tunately, the door stood open, and he slipped through, and then **over** the faggots into the newly-fallen snow, where he lay quite exhausted.

But it would be too painful to tell of all the privations and misery that the duckling endured during the severe weather. He was lying in a marsh, among the reeds, when the sun again began to shine. The larks were singing, and the spring had set in in all its beauty.

The duckling now felt able to flap his wings. They rustled much louder than before, and bore him away most sturdily ; and before he was well aware of it he found himself in a large garden, where the apple-trees were in full blossom, and the fragrant elder was steeping its long drooping branches in the waters of a winding canal.

Three magnificent white swans now emerged from the thicket before him : they flapped their wings, and then swam lightly on the surface of the water.

"I will fly towards those royal birds—and they will strike me dead for daring to approach them, so ugly as I am ! But it matters not. Better far to be killed by them than to be pecked at by the ducks, beaten by the hens, pushed about by the girl who feeds the poultry, and to suffer want in the winter." And he flew into the water, and swam towards those splendid swans, who rushed to meet him with rustling wings the moment they saw him. "Do but kill me !" said the poor animal, as he bent his head down to the surface of the water and awaited his doom. But what did he see in the clear stream ? Why, his own image, which was no longer that of a heavy-looking dark grey bird, ugly and ill-favoured, but of a beautiful swan !

It matters not being born in a duck-yard, when one is hatched from a swan's egg !

Some little children now came into the garden, and threw bread-

crumbs and corn into the water; and the youngest cried, "There is a new one!" The other children clapped their hands, and flew

to their father and mother, and they all said, "The new one is the prettiest."

He then felt quite ashamed, and hid his head under his wing.

He was more than happy, yet none the prouder, for a good heart is never proud. He remembered how he had been pursued and made game of; and now he heard everybody say he was the most beautiful of all the beautiful birds. He flapped his wings and raised his slender neck, as he cried in the fulness of his heart, "I never dreamed of such happiness while I was an Ugly Duckling."

DICK'S CAT AT COURT.

306

WHITTINGTON AND HIS CAT.

IN the reign of King Edward the Third there lived in a small country village a poor couple, named Whittington, who had a son called Dick. His parents dying when he was very young, he could scarcely remember them at all; and as he was not old enough to work, he was for a long time very badly off, until a kind but poor old woman took compassion on him, and made her little cottage his home. She always gave him good advice, made him industrious and well behaved, and he became quite a favourite in the village.

When he was fourteen years old, and had grown up to be a stout, good-looking lad, the good old woman died, and he had to look out how to earn his living by his own exertions. Now Dick was a boy of quick parts, and fond of gaining knowledge by asking questions of everybody who could tell him something useful. In this way he had heard much about the wonderful city of London; more, indeed, than was true, for the country folks were fond of talking of it as a place where the streets were paved with gold. This arose from their ignorance, for very few indeed among them had ever seen it. Although Dick was not such a ninny as to believe this nonsense, yet he felt very curious to go to London, and see it with his own eyes; hoping in so great and wealthy a place he should get on better than he could in a poor country village.

Accordingly, on a fine summer's morning he boldly started on his journey, with but a trifle of money in his pocket, yet full of good spirits and hope. When he had walked on for some hours, he felt extremely tired, and was rather alarmed at the difficulty that now stared him in the face: how was he to get over the ground? While he was seriously reflecting upon this, he heard the wheels of a heavy waggon, on its way to London, slowly advancing on the road behind him. This rough sound was like music to his ears, weary as he then was. As soon as the waggoner came up, Dick, without much ado, told him his plan, and begged that he might have a lift until his legs were sufficiently rested to let him walk again. This the man agreed to, and so, partly by riding, and partly by walking side by

side with the waggoner, Dick managed to reach the great city he
was so anxious to behold.

Though Dick's heart beat with joy on finding himself really in
London, he was a little disappointed at the look of the streets and
houses. He had fancied to himself a grander and richer sort of
place than the city seemed to him at first sight to be. But this is
a very common kind of mistake; indeed, we all of us make it sometimes. In our fancy, everything we have yet to see appears only
on its bright side; but, in reality, everything has its dark side as
well. Dick soon found out this truth from experience, as we shall
see presently.

After Dick had parted with the friendly waggoner, he had only a

groat left out of his little store of money : a night's lodging and a
scanty meal or two soon exhausted this, and after wandering about
for a whole day, he felt so weary and faint from fatigue and hunger,
that he threw himself down on the steps of a doorway, and resting
his head on this hard pillow, slept soundly until morning. Not
knowing what to do, he walked on farther, and, looking about him,
his eye fell on a curious-looking knocker, on the door of a large
house, just like the face of a blackamoor grinning. He could not
help grinning too, and then he began to think there could be no
great harm if he lifted the knocker, and waited to see who should
appear.

Now, the house stood in the Minories, and belonged to a worthy merchant of the name of Fitzwarren, who had a daughter called Alice, of about the same age as Dick. It was the cook, a sour-looking, ill-tempered woman, who opened the door. When she saw it was a poor worn-out-looking country lad who had disturbed her at breakfast, she began to abuse him roughly and to order him away. Luckily for Dick, Mr. Fitzwarren, who was a benevolent, courteous gentleman, came up to the door at this moment, and listened attentively to the poor lad's story; and so much struck was he with his truthful aspect and simple language, that he kindly ordered Dick to be taken into the house, and cared for, until he should be able to get his living in some decent way.

Alice, the merchant's daughter, who had overheard all this, and well knowing the unfeeling nature of the cook, did all she could to save Dick from her ill-will and harsh treatment. Her own kindness of heart made her feel for the distress of the poor orphan boy, and she tried her best to make her parents take some interest in his welfare. She succeeded so far, that they agreed Dick should remain in the house if he would make himself useful by assisting the cook, and in other ways. This, however, was not a very easy matter, for the cook never liked the boy from the first, and took every opportunity to spite him. Amongst her other acts of cruelty, she made him sleep on a wretched hard bed, placed in an old loft, sadly infested with rats and mice. Dick dared not to complain, and, besides, he did not like to make mischief; so he bore with this trouble as long as he could, and resolved at length, when he should have money enough, to buy himself a cat.

Now it happened that within a very few days from this, a poor woman passing by the door while he was cleaning it, offered to sell him a cat, and when she heard his story, let him have it for a penny. Dick took his prize up to his loft, and there kept Pussy in an old wicker basket with a cover to it, to be out of the cook's sight, as he feared she would do the cat a mischief, if she found her straying about. Now and then he would take Pussy with him when he went out on errands, so that they soon became great friends. Not only was Pussy a capital mouser, and very soon got rid of his nightly visitors, the rats and mice, but she was very clever and quick in learning many diverting tricks that her master tried to make her perform.

One day, when Dick was amusing himself with her antics, he was surprised by his young mistress Alice, who became afterwards almost as fond of the cat as Dick was himself. This young lady always remained the poor lad's friend, and this cheered him up

under the barbarous usage he received from the cook, who sometimes beat him severely. Alice was not beautiful in person, but,
what was of greater real value to her, she was truly amiable in disposition, and had the most agreeable manners. It was no wonder,
then, that Whittington, smarting under the ill-treatment of the
coarse cook-maid, should regard his kind young mistress as nothing
less than an angel; whilst the modesty of the youth, his correct
conduct, his respectful demeanour, and his love of truth, interested
Alice so much in his behalf, that she persuaded her father to let
one of the apprentices teach him to write—for he could already read
very well; and the progress he made in this, and in acquiring
further knowledge, was astonishing.

Mr. Fitzwarren, as we have said, was a merchant; and it was his
custom, whenever one of his ships went out, to call his family and

servants around him, and ask them all in turn to make a little venture, according to their wishes or abilities, under the particular
charge of the captain. Poor Whittington was the only one absent
when this next happened ; he, poor fellow, felt ashamed that he
possessed nothing of value to send as his venture. But he was called
for, and told that he must produce something—no matter what—to
try his luck. The poor youth then burst into tears, from very
vexation and shame ; when his kind friend Alice whispered in his
ear, " Send your cat, Dick," and forthwith he was ordered to take
Pussy, his faithful friend and companion, on board, and place her in
the hands of the captain. His young mistress, however, took good

care to make the mouser's good qualities known to the captain, so that he might make the most of her for Dick's benefit.

After the loss of his cat Dick felt rather sorrowful, and this was not lessened by the taunts and jeers of his old enemy, the cook, who used to tease him constantly about his "fine venture," and the great fortune he was to make by it. Poor fellow! she led him a miserable life; and as his young mistress, besides, was soon after absent from home on a visit, he lost heart entirely, and could no longer bear to live in the same house with his tormentor.

In this gloomy state of mind, he resolved to quit Mr. Fitzwarren's house, and started off accordingly one morning very early, unobserved by any one, and wandered out of town until he reached the foot of Highgate Hill, just beyond Holloway. Tired and wretched, he flung himself upon a large stone by the roadside, which, from his having rested himself upon it, is called WHITTINGTON'S STONE to this day. He presently sank into a sort of doze, from which he was roused by the sound of Bow bells, that began to ring a peal, as it was Allhallows Day. As he listened to them, he fancied he could make out the following words, addressed to himself, and the more he listened the plainer the bells seemed to chant them to his ear:

> " TURN AGAIN, WHITTINGTON,
> LORD MAYOR OF LONDON."

A new spirit of hope was awakened within him as he kept repeating these words after the bells, for they inspired him with great thoughts. So distinctly did they appear to be addressed to him, that he was resolved to bear any hardships rather than check his way to fortune by idle repining. So he made the best of his way home again, and, late in the morning as it was, he luckily got into the house without his absence having been noticed.

Like a brave-hearted boy, he exerted himself now more than ever to make himself useful, especially to his worthy master and his kind young mistress, and he succeeded beyond his expectation ; almost everybody saw that he was desirous of doing his duty, and to excel in all he attempted to do. Alice was more and more satisfied with his conduct and behaviour, and heard with pleasure of the great progress he was making in his studies. But the cook continued as surly as ever, although she must have seen he no longer minded her ill-temper as he used to do.

While matters were thus going on at home, Mr. Fitzwarren's ship, the " Unicorn," was slowly pursuing her voyage to a distant part of Africa. In those days the art of navigation was but little understood, and much greater dangers were incurred through ignorance in steering vessels than is now the case. The " Unicorn " was unlucky enough to meet with much foul weather, and was so tossed about that she lost her latitude ; but what was worse, owing to her being so long away from any port, her provisions were nearly exhausted, and all on board began to despair of their ever returning to England. It was wonderful that all through this dreadful period of suffering, Whittington's cat should have been kept alive and well; but so it was, and this no doubt was owing to the great care taken of her by the captain himself, who had not forgotten the interest

Alice had expressed to him about the cat. Not only was Pussy by this means preserved from death, but she contrived to bring up a little family of kittens that she had during the voyage: their funny tricks greatly diverted the sailors, and helped to keep them in good humour when they began to feel discontented.

At length, when the last biscuit had been eaten, and nothing but destruction seemed to be in store for the poor mariners, they were rejoiced to find that their prayers to heaven for deliverance had been heard; for when day broke, land was descried. This proved to be a kingdom on the African coast abounding with wealth. The inhabitants, who were chiefly copper-coloured, were hospitable, and much pleased to be visited by the ships of white men, for the cruel slave-trade had not then been introduced among them. The King, as soon as he heard of the arrival of the "Unicorn," sent some of his great men to invite the captain and a few of his companions to visit his Court, and to have the honour of dining with him and his Queen.

A grand dinner, in the fashion of the country, was provided for the occasion; and great good humour and cordiality prevailed until the dishes were placed on the table, when the white visitors were astonished at the appearance of rats and mice in vast numbers, which came from their hiding-places, and devoured nearly all the viands in a very short time. The King and Queen seemed to regard this as no uncommon event, although they felt quite ashamed it should occur on this occasion.

When the captain found, on making inquiry, that there was no such animal as a cat known in the country, he all at once thought of asking permission to introduce Whittington's cat at Court, feeling convinced that Pussy would soon get rid of the abominable rats and mice that infested it. The royal pair and the whole Court listened to the captain's account of the cat's good qualities as a mouser with wonder and delight, and were impatient to see her talents put to the proof. Puss was accordingly taken ashore in her wicker basket, and a fresh repast having been prepared, which on being served up was about to be attacked in a similar way to the previous one, she sprang in a moment among the crowd of rats and mice, killing several, and putting the rest to flight in less than the space of a minute.

Nothing could exceed the satisfaction caused by this event. The King and Queen and all the courtiers did not know how to make enough of Pussy, and they became more and more fond of her when they found how gentle and playful she could be with them, notwithstanding her fierceness in battling with rats and mice. As might be expected, the captain was much pressed to leave this valuable cat with his black friends, and he, thinking that they would no doubt make a right royal return for so precious a gift, readily acceded to the request. The Queen's attachment to Puss seemed to know no bounds, and she felt great alarm lest any accident should befall her, fearing that in that case the odious rats and mice would return more ferocious than ever. The captain comforted her greatly, however, by assuring her that Pussy had a young family of kittens on board, which should also be duly presented at Court.

Now the Queen had a tender heart, and when she had heard from the captain all the particulars of Whittington's story, and of the poor lad's great regret at parting with his cat, she felt quite loth to deprive him of his favourite, especially when Pussy's kittens were found to be quite able to frighten away the rats and mice. So the cat was replaced in her wicker basket, and taken on board again. The gratitude of the King and Queen for the important services rendered by Pussy and her family was manifested in the rich treasures they sent to Whittington as the owner of the wonderful cat.

The captain, having at last completed his business and refitted his ship as well as he could, took leave of his African friends, and set sail for England ; and after a very long absence, during which Mr. Fitzwarren had given up the ship for lost, she safely arrived in the port of London. When the captain called upon the merchant, the latter was much affected at again beholding so valued a friend restored to him whom he regarded as lost ; the ladies also who were present wept for joy, and were very curious to hear of the perils encountered and the strange sights witnessed by the captain. Alice, in particular, wanted to know without delay what had befallen Dick's cat, and what was the success of his venture. When the captain had explained all that happened, he added that Whittington ought to be told of the result of his venture very cautiously, otherwise his good luck might make him lose his wits. But Mr. Fitzwarren would hear of no delay, and had him sent for at once.

Poor Dick at that moment had just been basted by the cook with a ladle of dripping, and was quite ashamed to appear in such a plight before company. But all his woes were soon forgotten when the worthy merchant told him of his good fortune, and especially when he added that it was a just reward granted by Heaven for his patience under hard trials, and for his good conduct

and industry. When the boxes and bales containing the treasures given by the African King and Queen to the owner of the cat, and marked outside with a large W, were displayed before the astonished youth, he burst into tears, and implored his master to take all if he would but continue to be his friend. But the merchant would touch none of it, declaring it to belong to Whittington, and to him alone.

Before the captain took his leave, he said to Dick playfully, " I have another present for you from the African Queen," and calling to a sailor below, ordered him to bring up the wicker basket, out of which leaped Mrs. Puss, to the great joy of her former master; and right happy was she to see him again, purring round him, and

rubbing her head against his face when he took her up in his arms.
For the rest of her days she continued to live with her grateful
master.

Dick made a liberal and proper use of his wealth, rewarding all
who had been in any way kind to him; nor did he even omit his
old enemy the cook when bestowing his bounty, although she could
never after look him full in the face from a sense of shame.   Mr.
Fitzwarren constantly refused Whittington's earnest wishes that he
would accept at least some of his great wealth, but he agreed to
become his guardian and the manager of his property until he
should be of age.   Under his prudent counsel Whittington grew
up to be a thriving merchant, and a wise and good citizen.   With

all this success he never lost his old modesty of behaviour; and
deeply as he loved Alice, he for a long time delayed to make his
secret known to her father, lest he should be thought presumptuous;
but the kind merchant had long suspected the fact, and at last
taxed Richard with it. He could not deny it, but found he had
no cause to regret having opened his heart to Mr. Fitzwarren. That
worthy man, on Whittington's coming of age, rewarded him with
the hand of his daughter, who fully shared his love, having long
secretely regarded him with favour.

Whittington rose in eminence every year, and was universally
esteemed. He served in Parliament, was knighted also, and was
thrice Lord Mayor of London; thus fulfilling the prophecy uttered,
as he had fancied, by Bow bells. When he served that office for
the third time, it was during the reign of Harry the Fifth, just
after that great King had conquered France. Sir Richard entertained him and his Queen in such great style that the King was
pleased to say, "Never Prince had such a subject!" to which it
has been said the Lord Mayor loyally replied, "Never subject had
such a Prince!"

At this entertainment the King was much pleased with a fire

made from choice woods and fragrant spices, upon which Sir Richard said he would add something that would make the fire burn more brightly for the pleasure of his sovereign, when he threw into the flames various bonds given by the King for money borrowed of the citizens to carry on the war with France, and which Sir Richard had called in and discharged, to the amount of sixty thousand pounds—to the admiration of all who witnessed this act of patriotic generosity.

After a long life, this good man, who nobly distinguished himself by public works and acts of charity—by many of which he is still kept in memory—died, universally regretted, having survived Alice, his wife, about twenty years.